Through the Darkness

Erin O'Reilly

Affinity
eBook Press
NZ

2014

Through the Darkness
© Erin O'Reilly 2014

Affinity E-Book Press NZ LTD
Canterbury, New Zealand

ISBN: 978-1-927282-29-8

Editor: Nat Burns
Cover Design: Irish Dragon Designs
Photo Credit: Bill Long Photography

Acknowledgements

First, I want to thank Julie for all her help getting this story off the ground and advising me every time I couldn't think of where to go next.

Secondly, I want to thank Mary Hettel for reading this manuscript and pointing out where I needed to change things.

Next, I'd like to thank Nancy for volunteering to read the final copy.

Thank you Nat for your excellent editing.

Finally, I'd like to thank Affinity eBook for publishing *Through the Darkness*.

Dedication

For Julie and Nancy
Even in my darkest moments, you both have been there for
me.

Other Books by the Author

Revelations
Deception
Fearless
'55 Ford
Fractured
Specter of Fear
Wolf at the Door
Sandcastles

Written With JM Dragon

Earthbound
New Beginnings
Atonement
Quest on Behalf of Love
Echoes of the Past
Paradox of Love
The End Game

Table of Contents

Chapter One

People often chided Becca Cameron for making the thirty-five mile drive one-way to get to her job in Denver but she'd given up listening to them. She actually relished the silence or maybe some soft classical music after a hectic day of being a project manager's personal assistant.

She flicked on the high beams as she traveled down the darkened highway toward home. It was fall, rutting season for deer and she knew that at any moment a deer could come dashing out of nowhere and across the road.

Once her car climbed to the top of the final rise, she saw a flashing yellow light in the distance and beyond that, the bright lights of an overpass. She would be home in less than fifteen minutes, barring any deer darting in front of her truck.

Becca's eyes fixed on the flashing yellow light, knowing that the roadway that justified the warning light was little more than a right hand turn onto a dirt road rutted by rain. Twice a day she passed under the light and looked down Hanging Tree Lane. Often she would find herself pressing the brake pedal and creeping past the thoroughfare, intrigued by the silent, seemingly neglected road. The pull she felt to explore the road farther was, at times, so overwhelming that she had to grip the steering wheel tight so as not to follow that path not taken. Tonight though, she sped on by, barely giving it a glance as she concentrated on the flashes of lightning in the distance.

†

The sheer power of the loud claps of thunder startled Becca as she turned down the dirt road that led to her home. Once she'd pulled into the garage, which was also a shed, Becca quickly collected her briefcase, purse and lunch bag before dashing the fifteen feet to the porch. Just as she stepped a foot on the wraparound porch, big sloppy drops of rain began to fall.

The click of the door behind her made Becca sigh happily as she dropped her belongings and crouched down to greet her dog, a cockapoo named Georgette.

"Home at last, girl."

She listened to the rain pelting the porch roof. "And, just in time it would seem. How was your day, Georgie? Did Gwen spoil you rotten again?"

She stood and closed her eyes as the smell of polish, wood, and beef stew filled her nostrils. Georgie ran past her as she was walking to the kitchen and sat in front of the stove with her stubby tail wagging.

"Yum, that smells delicious."

Becca pulled open the oven door, put on a kitchen mitt and carefully pulled the cast iron Dutch oven out before settling it on the stovetop. Her mouth was watering as she lifted the lid and saw the scrumptious meal.

"There's enough here for lunch tomorrow, too."

Georgie was sitting by her side, thumping her tail, and whining.

Becca laughed. "You're spoiled and I shouldn't give you a piece of this but I will once it cools off."

After getting a glass of Pinot Noir and a sizable slice of the bread that Gwen had baked, Becca made her way to the table with her bowl of stew, listening as the rain turned to softer drops.

"Once it stops, I'll let you out one more time."

She blew on a chunk of meat before tossing it to her dog.

†

In the deer stand a mere fifty yards away, a figure studied the house. The housekeeper never set the alarm so it had been easy to gain entry once she left. The meal cooking on the stove had smelled wonderful and the watcher had added a few extra herbs and spices to the stew.

Luckily, Georgette was laid-back. They had met on many occasions and the dog did not consider the visitor an intruder.

With quick purpose, the stranger had climbed the stairs two at a time, then opened the door at the top of the staircase. After lifting the mattress, one sachet had been removed and a different sachet of herbs placed in the center before the mattress was lowered and the covers smoothed.

Back at the front door, the watcher had looked around the interior. Once satisfied that all was as it should be, the intruder had walked outside. The sky with frequent lightning and thunder caused the watcher to run for the deer stand where it was dry.

From the perch, the figure had concentrated on the darkness of the dirt road leading to the house, willing Becca to arrive home before the rain started. When the headlights brightened the dark night, the watcher had let out an audible sigh of relief.

For the next two hours, vigilant eyes watched the house as Becca moved about. When the light in the upstairs bedroom went on at nine, just as it did every night, the watcher knew it wouldn't be much longer before Becca finished her nightly ritual.

At first, it had spooked the watcher when Becca stood at the window and appeared to be looking right at the deer stand. But this had happened every night for the past year and the watcher now knew to wait until Becca placed her palm on the windowpane and closed her eyes. Then, within a few minutes, the light always went out.

Then, as every night, thirty minutes later, the watcher climbed down the deer stand's ladder and followed a narrow path toward home.

Chapter Two

Becca smiled but didn't open her eyes when she heard the sound of Massenet's "Meditation" from Thais nudging her gently awake. She knew she had until Delibes's Flower Duet finished to lay there and enjoy the music. It had been a long time since she'd slept so deeply and the nightmares that usually frequented her night hadn't materialized. Becca was at peace with herself and the world.

That's an odd feeling, she told herself.

Georgette bounded onto the bed and began prodding Becca with her cold, wet nose.

"Not yet, girl. The flower hasn't played yet. You know you can't go out before we hear the woman sing."

Not long after, Becca was making her way down the stairs to open the back door for her dog. While Georgette romped in the walled in yard, Becca poured herself a cup of coffee, grabbed a banana and sat on one of the kitchen chairs. The sense of peace still surrounded her and for the first time since the accident, she could remember what had happened and not have the sinking feeling that her life would never right itself.

Her eyes tracked to the wall clock and noted it was six o'clock and still dark outside. Georgie was scratching and barking at the door.

When Becca opened the door, the dog bounded into the house, skidded across the floor to her food bowl, and sat with her tail thumping on the floor.

"Don't worry, girl, I won't forget to feed you." Becca ruffled the dog's head as she poured some dry dog food in the bowl, then filled the water bowl.

"There you go, all set for the day. Now, if I don't get a move on, I'm going to be late for work and Mr. Douglas won't be happy with me."

†

The morning was glorious and Becca savored every moment of the peace that the good night's sleep had brought her. Driving toward the east, she watched as the sun began its slow journey above the horizon. Blue, the color of robin eggs, mixed with purples and darker blues before the entire sky turned white, just before the sun heralded the new day.

Becca pushed the visor down just as she came to the flashing light and Hanging Tree Lane. No one was behind her, so she stepped on the brake and stopped. Rain from the night before dotted the weeds, making them seem to shine like diamonds as the newly risen sun's rays fell on them. In an instant, the moment was gone and Becca smiled.

"One day I will put my truck in four wheel drive and see what's down there," she told herself.

Her phone rang and Becca pushed the Bluetooth button.

"Becca Cameron." She glanced at the clock—six-forty-five.

"Where are you?"

"I am on my way in now, sir. I will arrive at seven thirty, which is my usual time.

"I don't care about that, Cameron, your hours are what I tell you they are."

"I believe that when I started working for Eastman, HR told me my hours are from eight to four, Mr. Douglas."

Becca gritted her teeth.

"Your responsibility is to be here when I am and not when you feel like arriving."

"Excuse me, Mr. Douglas, I already give the job two hours of free time. What more can you possibly ask of me?" Becca felt her shoulders stiffen.

"If you want to continue being my personal assistant, Cameron, I suggest you set your hours accordingly."

Becca bit the inside of her cheek to keep her anger in check.

"Mr. Douglas, I suggest that if you want me to work more than the required eight hours—please note that I work more like ten hours a day for you—then you should find a way to pay me for the extra hours."

"Ten hours or eighteen hours it makes no difference to me. *I* want you here when *I* get in."

"In that case, you may want to find someone else for the job. My contract specifies that I work eight hours a day for the salary I receive. Perhaps I should go to HR and see what they can do."

"Don't you threaten me, Cameron, it won't bode well for you if you do."

The connection ended abruptly and Becca punched the hands free button to disable it before she growled. During the past three years that she had worked as Douglas's PA, they had the same discussion at least once a month.

"I won't let him ruin my good mood." Becca said aloud, smiling. "I don't know what changed to make me feel this way, but I won't let Mr. Sourpuss ruin my day."

†

With a smile still on her face, Becca checked her watch as she stood in front of the elevator doors waiting for them to open. Unless the elevator stopped in mid-ascent, she would be in her office at her usual seven-thirty. The traffic was so light; she'd thought for a moment that it must be a holiday.

When the doors opened, Becca made her way to the back of the elevator and waited for others to crowd their way into the small enclosure. She chuckled silently as a hand held open the elevator doors just before they closed. It never failed that the same woman would always just get to the elevator car right before it closed. The woman was nondescript and dressed in a bulky brown overcoat, making it difficult to tell if she was lean or chunky. The woman always stood in front of the row of floor buttons with a knit cap pulled on her bent head making eye contact with no one.

As the elevator ascended, people got off and eventually it was just Becca and the odd woman left.

"Have a good day," Becca said, just as she did every day, when the chime sounded for her floor.

And, as always, she had to strain to hear the woman's whisper. "You too."

†

Jim Douglas, her immediate boss and the project manager for Eastman was on Becca just as she inserted her keycard into her door's lock.

"Finally, you're here. Have you forgotten that we have a meeting at eight-fifteen?"

His face was beet red and Becca saw veins popping on his neck.

Becca smiled and nodded as she unlocked and pushed her office door open.

"No, I haven't forgotten, Mr. Douglas. If you will give me a moment to get settled, I will give you the up-to-date data you will need for your presentation."

"You should have given *that* to me yesterday, Cameron. Now you've left me with only a short time to prepare."

"Did you check your email?"

"Why would I? I expected all the information I needed on my desk two days ago," he sneered. "I've told you repeatedly how I want you to deliver information to me yet you still do it your way."

Douglas stepped closer to Becca.

"*I* am the boss here not you, Cameron. Is that clear?"

"Abundantly."

Becca took a step back.

"You were out of your office and I thought the information was too sensitive to just put on your desk. So, I sent you all the details just after lunch yesterday and I put the hard copy in the Knox folder in the filing cabinet in your office. Had you read your email, you would have found all the information you needed."

"Just be in my office to brief me in two minutes," he ordered. "Incompetence will not be tolerated, Cameron. You are not in some satellite office. You're at the corporate headquarters and damn lucky to be here. If you don't stop your careless ways you will find yourself out of a job."

He turned away only to turn back around.

"There are lots of unemployed PA's out there who'd do your job how *I* want it done," he said. "It's something for you to think about, Cameron."

✝

Becca watched the man leave and could feel a crack in her good mood—one that was threatening to expand.

I can't believe that I spent all those years earning my MBA to end up some nincompoop's lackey. I can't wait for this project to end so I can take some days off, she thought angrily.

She made her way to her desk, pulled out her chair, and sat.

I won't let him ruin my day.

Becca picked up her phone, dialed a number from memory, and waited to hear the familiar voice.

"Hey, Kim, what are you doing for lunch?"

Becca smiled as Kim responded.

"I'll see you at our usual bench then. Bye"

With a quick glance at the door across the hallway, Becca sighed.

Now to deal with him. I really need to speak with HR and find another PA position.

Becca regularly thought about seeking a new job within the company but always hesitated. There was no way she would leave the rest of the team to cope with her boss' anger and demands. She had done a good job running interference for them and would continue to do so.

Becca stood, straightened her back, and, with resolve, walked to the office across from hers.

✝

The sun warmed the cool air as Becca blew on a spoonful of the stew she'd warmed before going outside to the park across from the Eastman parking area.

"Well, that looks scrumptious," Kim said as she approached.

"It is. Wanna bite?"

"Did you make it?" The tall slender redhead eyed Becca.

"No. You know Gwen did."

"Well in that case, yes, I'd like to taste it."

Becca held out the spoonful of stew to Kim who slurped it into her mouth.

"Wow, I wish I had someone to cook for me." Kim said as she settled down next to her friend.

Becca laughed. "Once a week is all I get. The rest of the time, I am left to my own devices."

"That, my dear, is why you have the killer body that you insist on hiding behind your outdated sixties look."

Kim took a sandwich from her bag, unwrapped it and took a bite.

"You'll never find anyone dateable in that getup."

Becca didn't make eye contact.

. It's been more than a year, Becca. It's time that you move on."

"But it hasn't been a year," Becca whispered.

"Oh, my sweet adorable friend, it is time. You work too many hours, then you drive home to what…a big old rambling house sitting on two hundred and fifty acres with only Georgie for company."

"My great-grandfather built that house. Those six inch walls keep it cool in the summer and warm in the winter."

Becca paused and sighed. "It's the only home I've known and it is the only place that I feel truly safe."

Kim squeezed Becca's hand.

"What if I brought an overnight bag with me tomorrow and we spend the weekend together. Would you like that? We could watch old movies and pig out on popcorn and ice cream. I'll bring everything."

"I'd like that."

After a moment of silence, Becca scratched her neck and closed her eyes. "What kind of ice cream?"

Kim laughed. "You already know the answer to that one."

"Birthday cake?"

Becca giggled and hugged Kim. "You're too good to me."

Becca took a bite of stew and let the unspoken silence have its say.

"Now tell me about your boss crabapple," Kim said breaking the silence.

"We've worked on nothing but the Knox project and the completion date is in two weeks. The team is way ahead of schedule and we should have the final presentation done and to Mr. Douglas earlier than expected."

Becca took another bite, chewed, and continued. "As for Mr. Douglas, it seems as though he thinks that the louder he yells at me the more I will do. If it weren't for the team, I'd find another job."

"You work ten to twelve hours a day as it is…doesn't he know that?"

Kim took a bite of her sandwich and chewed it slowly.

"You should go talk to HR," Kim advised and grinned. "But by all means, avoid talking to the VP of Acquisitions. From what I hear, she is not a very nice person."

Becca shrugged.

"All of them, including Mr. Eastman himself, are supposedly readily available for the employees. Besides, I'm not sure anyone gets to be a vice president by being nice. As I've noticed during the past three years, most people will claw and climb their way to get a promotion. Loyalty is a lost art I think."

Becca shoved her stew away.

"He called me before seven this morning asking why I wasn't at work yet. Once again, I told him he could find someone else."

"No way." Kim's eyes widened.

"Yes, way. I told him I was thinking about speaking with HR."

"Bet that shut him up."

Becca shook her head.

"It did…he hung up on me. He didn't take me up on my offer and I haven't spoken to HR."

Kim shook her head and let out a sarcastic laugh.

"You know that he does this same dance every time a deadline draws near. I just try to fly under his radar…it hasn't worked."

Becca screwed the top of her thermos on and smiled at her friend.

"Perhaps one day he will surprise me and give the team one word of appreciation. But I won't hold my breath."

"You deserve better, Becca…you need more down time so you can do something other than drive to work, do your job, and then drive back home only to go to bed early."

"I'm going to take a few days off the week after Knox is finished," Becca said.

"Great. Where are you going?"

"Nowhere, really. With winter approaching there are things I need to fix."

Kim laughed. "Only you would take vacation and stay home."

Silence ensued as they collected their belongings.

"I miss her so much," Becca whispered.

"I know you do, sweetie."

Kim put her arm around Becca's shoulders and pulled her close. "You need to get away from that house and the memories it holds."

She kissed Becca's cheek. "I'm here for you."

The tears that always threatened whenever Becca spoke or thought about what had happened didn't materialize. The sense of peace that filled her when she woke that morning was still with her.

"Thank you." Becca pulled away from Kim and picked up her belongings. "I need to get back to work."

"Yeah, me too. So we are on for the weekend right?" Kim asked.

Becca smiled. "I'm looking forward to it."

Chapter Three

The watcher paced the small floor of the deer stand. It was almost eight and there was no sign of Becca. *She's never this late. God, I pray she hasn't been in an accident.*

Five minutes later, headlights illuminated the road leading to the house. The watcher let out a sigh of relief until the second set of headlights followed the first.

With great interest, the watcher saw Becca's car pull into the shed and the second car stop behind it. When the person emerged from the second car, the watcher scowled. Becca got out of her vehicle, went to the new arrival and hugged her close.

No! No, that can't be. The watcher saw the other woman open the trunk of her car and pull out an overnight bag. *No, I don't believe it…it can't be. Becca finished with her a year ago. Doesn't she know she isn't the right one?*

For the next two hours, the watcher observed the activities inside the home. It appeared that the two women were having a sleepover. Then, at around ten, all the downstairs lights went out and Becca's bedroom light went on. The watcher couldn't see all the bedroom windows but knew that only the bedrooms on this side of the house were used, and only one light was on. With a sinking feeling, the watcher dropped to the floor and looked at Becca standing in the window with her hand on the glass pane just as she did every night.

In an involuntary move, the watcher lifted a hand and put it against the side of the deer stand. *I hear you.*

When the interloper who had once been Becca's lover, came into view, she wrapped her arms around Becca's waist and nuzzled her neck. The watcher's hand dropped. It took every bit of the watcher's resolve to hold back the flood of tears that threatened when Becca turned in the woman's arms, and stood motionless before walking toward the bed.

"No, Becca, this is all wrong." The watcher said, pounding the floor of the deer stand. "How can this be happening? It is not as it should be. What will I do now?"

Blinded by tears, the watcher scrambled down the deer stand's ladder and walked along the narrow deer path heedless of being quiet. In the distance, Georgette barked. Refusing to look back at the house, long strides took the watcher away from the property.

✝

Once Becca made sure she locked all the doors, she took Kim's hand as they both climbed the stairs.

"You can sleep in the room across from the bathroom, Kim. There are fresh towels in the linen closet there."

"It's been a long time since I've been up here." Kim ran a fingernail down Becca's arm. "I remember our good times."

"I remember those too." Becca shrugged. "Time changes people. I'll see you in the morning."

She gave Kim a brief hug before entering her room.

✝

Dressed in boxers and a T-shirt, Becca stood in front of the window and splayed her fingers against the glass. Her eyes strained to pick out the old deer stand and memories flooded her mind.

"Where are you," she whispered. She closed her eyes and prayed. *Dear Lord, please hear my voice and bring love to my lonely life…*

Kim's arms encircled her waist and she kissed Becca's neck. "Just like old times."

Becca opened her eyes and turned in Kim's arms. "Not exactly like old times, Kim. I remember the bad more than the good. We made lousy partners and no matter how good the sex was, the rest of it overshadows everything. We are better at friendship than as lovers. I thought that we agreed on that."

Kim rested her forehead against Becca's and she let out a long sigh. "I know. Can we just hold one another while we sleep?"

Becca wrestled with what to say. "I don't know if I can trust you but it would feel good to have someone holding me tonight," she admitted finally.

"You can trust me," Kim whispered. "I can see it in your eyes how much you hurt." She frowned. "I wish there was something I could do to take the pain away."

"It's my own private hell and no one else can enter." Becca moved out of Kim's embrace. "Come on it is getting late and I'm bushed."

"If I promise to be good can I sleep with you?"

Becca raised an eyebrow.

"Nothing sexual I promise." Kim drew in a breath. "I just want to feel close to you. That's all I'll do and nothing more."

"Okay, but you have to stay on your side of the bed. Agreed?"

"Agreed."

✝

Eyes flew open when Becca felt an arm around her and someone spooning behind her. *Kim.* She mentally checked that she wasn't naked and let out a sigh of relief. *Yeah, Kim spent the night.* The presence of another woman in her bed, even if it was platonic, made her feel warm. It was now three nights in a row that she'd slept through a dreamless night, waking up happy and refreshed. She carefully moved out of the embrace and got out of bed.

Becca turned and watched Kim sleeping. *How beautiful she is. If only it had worked out between us...*

Memories of life with Kim filled her thoughts.

Their verbal exchanges during their many arguments were harsh, angry and nasty. Once the arguments were done, they would plead for forgiveness and swear it would never happen again. Then they would make an angry passionate type of love that was full of all the words that had passed between them. After one such session, Becca looked at Kim's naked body sprawled on the bed and knew they were through.

"We cannot go on like this, Kim. You need to find a place of your own."

Kim shook her head before getting up and heading for the bathroom.

Becca sat on the bed deciding whether to join Kim or dress. In the past, she would tell Kim they were done and then join her in a shower. This time she had dressed and left the room.

"I take it you meant what you said," Kim said as she entered the kitchen.

"Yes." Becca turned to face her lover. "I cannot go on like this."

"I promise...."

Becca held up her palm toward Kim. "Don't. We've both said those words before and we know they are meaningless. You need to find someone who you are more compatible with...we both know that isn't me."

"But I love you."

Becca moved toward Kim and placed her hand on Kim's cheek. "And, I love you but that isn't enough. I'm exhausted by the dance that we do and if truth be told, I am weary of you."

She kissed Kim's cheek. "And you are weary of me."

That had been two years earlier and here Kim was in her house again, singing as she came down the staircase. A smile crossed Becca's face as she turned and saw Kim in the doorway. "Did you sleep well?"

"As a matter of fact I did. I liked holding you...it made me feel at peace."

Becca's blue eyes fixed on Kim. "We won't go back there ever."

Kim smiled. "I know that, Becca, honest I do. I just liked feeling you close." She lifted one shoulder. "You ground me."

"Please don't do this and make me regret allowing you to come here." Becca's hands were shaking and she stuffed them in her pocket. "Perhaps it would be best if you left after breakfast."

"You have it all wrong." Kim moved closer. "I do still love you but as a friend and nothing more. In the middle of the night, I woke when Georgie barked and I saw you sleeping in my arms. What I felt was love. Not the sexual kind but the kind that comes from a strong bond of mutual caring about one another."

She pulled Becca close to her. "Haven't we already both agreed that we make great friends and lousy lovers."

Becca stepped out of the embrace. "I was about to go collect fresh eggs for breakfast. You can help if you like."

"The last time I did, that big chicken began pecking at my hand." Kim laughed. "But since you asked so nicely, I'll give it another try."

Becca lightly punched Kim's arm and grinned. "That's the spirit we don't want it to get around that you're afraid of a chicken."

Kim giggled. "And just how would anyone else know."

With a wink, Becca said, "I'll tell them."

"Cruel, Becca Cameron, very very cruel."

Becca wrapped an arm around Kim's shoulders. "Don't worry, your secret is safe with me."

†

The rest of the weekend was pleasurable. Saturday they took Becca's truck around her property and stopped in a meadow by a pond for a picnic. That night they watched both the original and the remake of *The End of the Affair*.

"So what did you think?" Becca asked.

"There is something to be said for the black and white version. Somehow, the actors seem more real in black and white." Kim took a sip of her drink. "Although I did think that the lead actors seemed a bit bland… but the supporting cast made up for that I think."

"Why do you say that? I saw your eyes riveted on the screen."

"Don't get me wrong, I think the story itself was compelling…" Kim shrugged. "I guess I expected more out of them."

"So what about the remake?" Becca asked.

"At first, I thought it would rely on more glitz since it was set in World War Two. Any movie Julianne Moore is in I want to watch. She *is* hot."

Becca nodded. "That she is. Did you know she got an Academy Award nomination for the movie? But don't you think Deborah Kerr has a presence and a grace that very few actresses have today?"

"I guess I think that when they made the original the actors had to rely on their skills as actors and not so much on the added dramatic effects they have in today's movies."

"I agree. I thought that the black and white movie was more satisfying since it focused more on the affair."

"In both versions though, it was a great love story. To think she sacrificed so much for him." Kim let out a deep sigh. "I can only imagine a love like that."

"Someday we will both find it, Kim."

That night, when Becca stood in front of the window with her hand to the pane, Kim did not join her. *God, I know she's out there...please help us find one another.* That night, Kim held her again as she slept and the nightmares stayed away.

†

The watcher was glad when Becca came to the window alone that night. The annoying redhead was still in the house. *At least she isn't with her tonight. Becca obviously came to her senses and realized that the woman is bad news for her.* Once the light went out in Becca's bedroom, the watcher sighed—all was as it should be again.

†

The weekend with Kim was exactly what Becca needed—down time filled with laughter and companionship. She hadn't realized how much she missed hearing laughter, music, and the various sounds of other living beings in her house. And though she enjoyed Kim's company, she knew that she wanted something else. *No. I want someone else.*

Once Kim had left on Sunday, Becca turned on the television for some noise to blot out the silence she usually lived in. It was maddening for it only highlighted the fact that she was once again alone in the big old house, her only companions a black curly haired dog and the ghosts that lived there.

Chapter Four

A week later, the elevator doors slid open and Becca hesitated before gently elbowing her way to the back of the car. It was another week in a long series of weeks where she had no choice but kowtow to Jim Douglas and his berating words.

I need to do something about my situation with him. But what to do is the question. Once the Knox project is finished, I will seriously think about finding another position, she told herself as she boarded the elevator car.

The elevator car began its assent stopping at each floor allowing passengers to get out. When the door closed, Becca came to the sudden realization that she was alone. Caught up in her thoughts about the Knox project and its completion she hadn't realized that the woman whose hand always stopped the door from closing was not there.

Come to think of it, she hasn't been here all week. Becca's eyes narrowed. *Well there's a change. Maybe she's on vacation or she took a different elevator.*

When the car stopped at her floor, Becca exited and took one more pensive look inside, as if to make sure the woman really wasn't there.

I hope she's okay, she mused.

✝

The next two days flew by as Becca readied everything for the presentation of the Knox project. Her boss was more irritable than she'd ever known him to be. Everything was ready and even though they had a week to spare, he was still not satisfied, insisting that Becca go through everything numerous times.

Becca was busy rereading the proposal for the umpteenth time late Friday when she heard a soft knock on her door.

It must be one of the team, she thought warmly. *Mr. Douglas just opens the door.*

"Come in," she called.

When the door opened, Becca's jaw dropped open. Standing in the doorway was the most beautiful woman she had ever seen. She was dressed in black pants and an expensive charcoal gray jacket over a white silk shirt. Of course, Becca knew who the woman was and that made her stomach knot in anticipation of what was to come.

This can't be good.

"Please come in, Ms. Hunter."

"Good afternoon, Ms. Cameron. I tried Douglas's door but he seems to be gone."

"Yes, he usually leaves around noon on Fridays."

The woman arched an eyebrow. "Leaving you here to finish his work?"

Flustered, Becca looked away from the intense stare coming from blue gray eyes. "Is there something I can do to help you, Ms. Hunter?"

"You do know that it's almost six and everyone has left the building, don't you."

"Well, you're here too so I'm not the only one, Ms. Hunter."

Becca mentally slapped her own cheek. *That was a dumb thing to say. All I need is to be a smart ass to one of the big bosses.*

The grin that creased the woman's face unwittingly mesmerized Becca.

"My name is Chase," she said as she flicked back a strand of blonde hair.

"Oh, I could never call you by your first name." Becca looked up and wondered just how tall Chase Hunter was, her body seemed to go on forever. Her eyes took in the woman as a whole and realized that they were about the same height.

"Why not? May I call you Becca?"

"Of course you may use my first name but I need to show the proper respect for your position in the company and calling you by your first name wouldn't be right. Too familiar." Becca knew she was babbling but couldn't help the words from spilling out of her mouth. At the same time, the realization that the VP knew her first name rattled her.

"As of now you are off the clock, Becca, and have been for several hours now. That being said, you can call me Chase if you'd like."

"Thank you." Becca looked up at Chase's face. "Was that an order that I'm off the clock? Because..."

Chase moved and stood in front of Becca's desk. "Yes, it was. I've been watching this team for some time now and have noticed you arrive early and stay late. Don't you have someone to go home to?"

"Just George."

"Your husband?"

Becca grinned. "No. Georgette is my dog."

"Oh, I see." Chase rested the palms of her hands on the desk and leaned in. "I want to know why you are still here and your boss and team are not."

"The team usually works nine hours a day so I told them that on Fridays when Mr. Douglas leaves at noon they could too." Becca lost herself in the perfume that assailed her nose from the close proximity of Chase Hunter. "They don't get paid for the extra hours they put in. I thought it was equitable for them to leave early on Fridays."

"But not for you?"

"Ms. Hunter, they get paid a lot less than I do, it's the least I can do for them."

"Becca, does Jim Douglas know they leave too? Did you run it by him?"

Becca shook her head. "No. No, he doesn't know."

"Why?" Blue gray eyes fixed on Becca.

"Because it isn't something he'd ever think of doing. He told me to lead the team and make sure they do their jobs. I took that as putting me in charge of them."

Becca tried to look away—she couldn't. "I therefore made the decision that they leave when Mr. Douglas does on Friday."

For a long time, Chase said nothing but kept her eyes fixed on Becca. "I ask again. Why are you still here?"

Becca closed her eyes in an effort to hide from the intense scrutiny from across the desk. "Because, he will want this information first thing Monday morning...." Becca hesitated. "We, the team, have completed the Knox project and I am tying it all together while it is still fresh in my mind."

"Close down your computer, get your coat and things, and come with me, please."

Becca knew an order when she heard it although the *please* was a touch she rarely heard. "Can I at least finish up what I was doing?"

"No, upload the file to a flash drive and go home."

"You want me to work at home? That's ridiculous." Irritation colored Becca's voice. "I can stay here and get it all done and not have to worry about it."

"I don't want you to take it home. I want you to give it to me."

"But it's not finished."

"Becca, I understand that. Please upload the file and give it to me."

Conflicted and angry, Becca couldn't understand the reasoning behind the VP's request. More importantly, Becca would have to face her boss on Monday with an incomplete summary of the Knox project.

"Do not worry about what Jim Douglas will say or do. I will take care of him."

Becca reluctantly relaxed her shoulders.

"Now if you do the upload and get your belongings, I'd be pleased to treat you to dinner."

Becca's jaw dropped again. "Why?"

"To show my appreciation for the hard work you do."

Still mesmerized by the woman and her words, Becca did as requested. When she pulled on her coat, she looked expectantly at Chase.

"I will meet you in the lobby in ten minutes." Chase held out her hand. "The flash drive, please."

Becca robotically handed it to her and watched Chase walk out the door. She quickly made a copy of the document on another flash drive to take home and shut down her computer.

†

"This is a nice place. Do you eat here often?"

Chase smiled. "Some. I live alone and although I like to cook, I find it is the pits cooking for just me."

She watched Becca, as she had for as long as the young woman had worked for Eastman. Tonight had been the perfect opportunity to approach Becca and speak with her without the prying eyes of people like Douglas.

"Yeah, I know what you mean. I get one decent meal a week when my housekeeper comes. She makes me enough food for several days along with fresh baked bread. After that, I have to fend for myself. I'm not a bad cook I just don't like cooking for one. My freezer is loaded with quick, easy to prepare meals."

"You're lucky. Maybe I can use her too. It would be more personal than the cleaning service I have."

"I live thirty-five miles west of the city and I don't see Gwen driving that far for a job."

"But *you* do. Why?"

"It's my family home…I've never lived anywhere else except when I went to the university. Even then, I'd go home every chance I got."

"And that's why you applied at Eastman?'

The waiter arrived with a basket of mixed breads and two glasses of wine. He waited as Chase tasted the wine and poured them both a glass before he took their orders.

"I can recommend the pasta with shrimp. I've had it many times and it's a winner," Chase said.

She studied Becca. Auburn hair cascaded around her shoulders accentuating her very light blue eyes with a dark circle of blue around the pupil. *If the looks the men ogling her when we entered the restaurant is anything to go by, she is desirable to everyone.*

Becca shook her head.

"What? Is something wrong?" Chase frowned.

"No. I just can't get past the fact that I am having dinner with Eastman's Vice President of Acquisitions. It's so surreal to me."

"Surreal good or surreal bad?' Chase held her breath waiting for the answer.

"Definitely in a good way." Becca bit her bottom lip. "I've of course seen you in the building but I had no idea that I'd ever actually have a conversation with you, not to mention a personal one like this." Becca waved her hands.

"Will you answer a question for me?"

"Sure."

"Have you heard me referred to in a negative way?"

Becca knitted her eyebrows and shook her head. "I've never said anything detrimental about you." She shrugged. "I don't know you so how can I form an opinion. But I did hear that you weren't too nice but I didn't believe it. You are always smiling every time I've seen you."

"Hmm." Chase nodded and smiled at Becca before she held her hand out. "Give it.

"What?"

"The flash drive you copied after I left your office."

Becca's face flushed red. "How...."

"You are a conscientious worker." Chase grinned. "I'd have done the same."

Their meals arrived and they enjoyed the meal in companionable silence. Between courses, they talked about work and a little bit about their lives outside of work. Mentally Chase shook her head, realizing that they really didn't have hobbies or anything other than working for Eastman in common.

"To be perfectly frank, I really don't have much of a life outside of work," Becca said.

Chase grinned. "I was just thinking the same thing."

"Ah, a perfect pair then." Becca said, smiling. "To be honest, I stay late at work so I won't have to take it home with me. Home is the one place that I've decided is off limits to any work associated with my job."

"I hadn't thought of that option," Chase said. "I usually stuff my briefcase with work and finish it at home." She smiled. "No work at home...I like that concept."

"Give it a try. You might be surprised at how nice being away from work is."

Chase let out a hearty laugh. "I'd probably have signs of withdrawal...I've never done anything that radical."

Becca leaned in. "Trust me, you will find a whole new outlook on life."

"Okay, I'll give it a try and let you know."

†

Becca stood next to her truck and smiled at Chase. "Thank you for dinner. It was marvelous."

"The food?"

"No, silly. The food was great but the company was unexpectedly fabulous." Becca felt her cheeks heat and she looked away. "I'm sorry that was way out of line."

Chase tilted her head. "Not as far as I'm concerned. I feel exactly the same way. It was wonderful to actually eat a meal and have a beautiful woman sitting across from me who is well spoken and intelligent." She smiled. "Thank you for the company, Becca. It was an enjoyable evening for me."

"As it was for me. Well, I need to get going. Georgie is probably crossing her legs by now."

"Okay." Chase held out her hand. "Thank you for joining me— it was a delight."

Becca took Chase's hand and squeezed it gently. "The pleasure was all mine."

Chase lifted an eyebrow. "Not all yours." She squeezed Becca's hand in return. "I'll see you on Monday."

Becca watched Chase walk to her vehicle. *Of course, it's a BMW,* she noted.

She was all smiles as she got into her truck. "I hope I see you again, Chase Hunter," she said aloud.

Chapter Five

The meal with Chase on Friday had been a nice treat and to share it with a beautiful woman made it all the better. Becca found the VP to be quite funny and a genuinely nice person. Every time she thought of Chase during the weekend, she could feel her stomach flutter. She was definitely someone Becca wanted to see again.

She set her alarm clock to go off at five on Monday so she could get to her office and finish the report she knew Mr. Douglas would demand to see. On the drive in, she got as far as five miles past the flashing yellow light at Hanging Tree Lane before the rapidly moving traffic reached a standstill.

"Shit!" she slammed her hand on the steering wheel. Becca leaned her head out the window and saw there were only three vehicles ahead of her along with the flashing lights of emergency vehicles. She put her car in park, opened her door, and walked forward to get a better view of what was happening. An eighteen-wheeler was lying on its side with the back end of a car smashed under it. A woman was screaming frantically that her husband was still in the car.

"Why today of all days?" Becca muttered as she walked back toward her car. "Damn. Why did I let her take the files? I should have gone in yesterday just in case something like this happened."

An hour later, a lane opened and Becca crept by the overturned truck and saw a man lying on a stretcher as paramedics stood next to him. The woman was just standing there with her hands covering her face apparently sobbing. Blood covered the man's chest and head.

Becca sighed. "I bet he's dead, otherwise they'd be working on him and not just standing there."

It was at that moment that Becca realized just how fragile life was and how inconsequential the report was. *There by the grace of God, go I.*

†

As expected, Jim Douglas was standing in front of the elevator tapping his foot. "Do you know what time it is, Cameron?" He tapped his watch. "It is eight-twenty-one. Even by your standards you are twenty-one minutes late." He growled. "What do you have to say for yourself?"

"There was an accident that had me stopped for an hour. I sent you a text message and also left you a voice mail that I would be late."

"I'm not interested in excuses. You should have left early enough in case something like that happened. Your only saving grace is that the Knox report was on my desk this morning."

Becca frowned. Her stomach fluttered as she realized the only person who could have done that was Chase Hunter. "May I get by so I can go to my office?"

Douglas moved the bulk of a body just enough for Becca to get by.

"Thank you." Becca walked quickly to her office and once inside she put her things away and sat at her desk. A sealed envelope with her name on it was sitting in the middle of the desk. Becca picked it up and sliced it open. Unfolding the paper inside, she leaned back in her chair.

Becca,

Excellent report. I took the liberty of printing out a copy for Jim. Honestly, I didn't see what more you wanted to add. Keep up the good work.

C.H.

P.S. Thank you for having dinner with me. I had forgotten how delightful it is to have a meal with someone. Perhaps we can do it again soon. Call me. Let's set a date.

Becca grinned as she reread the postscript and caught a whiff of the perfume that Chase used.

She wants to have dinner with me again and she said the word date. Wow.

"I hope you aren't reading personal mail on company time." Jim Douglas stood in the doorway of Becca's office.

Becca's eyes trailed from the note to the man standing in front of her and she ignored his question. "What can I do for you, Mr. Douglas?"

"You need to go to the eighteenth floor with the presentation and show it to Hunter the VP of Acquisitions."

"I'm sorry, did I hear right? You want *me*," she touched her chest, "to present the Knox proposal and not *you?*"

"Are you now hard of hearing, Cameron? That is exactly what I said. Now get your notes and charts together and be on your way. Ms. Hunter is not someone you want to keep waiting."

Without saying anything else, Becca collected what she needed, stood, and walked out the door. Her boss followed her to the bank of elevators.

"Don't you go screwing this up for me, Cameron. She asked for you specifically, which tells me she is looking for grounds to delay or scrub the proposal. If that happens you will find yourself out of work."

†

The elevator doors slid smoothly open at the eighteenth floor and Becca walked through them. A woman with short brown hair, glasses and a ready smile looked up at Becca when she stepped into the reception area. The nameplate on the desk gave her name as Debra Kolinsky.

"Becca Cameron, to see Ms. Hunter."

The woman looked at her computer screen. "Ah, yes. There you are. Please have a seat." She pointed to the chairs to her left. "I will let Ms. Hunter know you're here."

Becca sat in one of the chairs that she found surprisingly comfortable. Compared to the chairs on her floor for visitors they were luxury personified. She was still trying to make sense of why she was there alone instead of at least alongside her boss. The fact that Chase asked specifically for her, along with the note she'd left on Becca's desk made her stomach flutter uncontrollably.

Becca remembered Jim Douglas' words about the reason for her going and she could feel her stomach start to churn. *If Chase is indeed looking to scrub the proposal, does that mean my job is in jeopardy?*

The only answer Becca could come up with was a resounding *yes* for that *was* what Mr. Douglas promised he'd do if the vice president scrapped the project.

"Ms. Cameron."

Becca looked up startled to see that the receptionist was standing in front of her. "Yes."

"Follow me and I'll take you to Ms. Hunter's office."

Becca stood and gave the woman a weak smile. She felt like a lamb being led to slaughter but the dinner she had shared with Chase gave her modicum of hope that wouldn't be fired. As she fell into step with the woman, Becca noticed Debra's shorter legs quickly ate up the distance until she stood in front of a door at the end of what seemed an endless corridor.

†

After a crisp knock on the door, a voice from inside, "Enter".

With her eyes closed, Becca willed herself to regain her composure.

"Ms. Hunter, Ms. Cameron, Mr. Douglas's PA."

Becca moved into the office and swallowed hard. The chair at the desk swiveled around and Chase's piercing eyes stared at her.

"Thanks, Debra."

Debra silently closed the door behind her as she exited the office.

"I have brought everything I need for the presentation of the Knox project. Where should I set up?"

When Becca heard no response, she looked directly at Chase. Again, she saw how exquisite Chase was. Her hair, the color of wheat, was in a knot at the back of her head and her sparkling eyes fixed only on her.

Chase pushed away from her desk and stood. "Good morning, Becca. It's good to see you again." She smiled. "I neglected to tell you the other night that your boss always praises you when we speak."

Becca took in Chase's body and again thought it was warm and inviting. "It's good to see you again too, Ms. Hunter. Unfortunately, I find that..."

"You find what, Becca."

Becca shook her head. "What I was going to say was out of line and certainly not professional."

"Okay, then I'm going to assume you were going to say something like *Mr. Douglas never speaks highly of me to my face*." Becca saw Chase's eyes search her face. "Is that about right?"

Becca nodded.

"I figured as much."

"Thank you for getting the file to Mr. Douglas. I appreciate it but it feels odd that you finished my work and sent it to him with my name on it."

Chase pointed to a chair in front of her desk. "Please take a seat."

Becca put the materials she was holding on the floor and then sat, expecting the vice president to sit behind her desk. Instead, she took the seat next to her. Becca swallowed hard. Just as Chase's facial features were attractive, she also had an elegant body—long, lean and oozing promises of what was to come. There was a raw sexuality about the woman's body.

"It is my job, Becca, to make sure that the part of Eastman that comes under my purview is running smoothly and that there are no problems. I have long suspected that the work that comes out of Jim Douglas' office doesn't come from him. That is one of the reasons I stopped by your office Friday evening."

"Ms. Hunter…."

"Chase."

"Not here." Becca let a slight smile appear. "Right now I feel I am in a damned if I do damned if I don't situation. How can I remain professional and answer your questions honestly?"

Chase pushed a loose piece of hair from her face. "It was not fair of me to ask those questions. I already know the answers. It is quite clear to me what is happening with you and your team."

Chase leaned back in her chair. "Since Knox is why I asked Douglas to send you up here, let's begin a dialogue about Knox."

"Okay. I think that what we've done with the Knox proposal is solid and should give the company a sizable profit."

Chase tapped her fingertips together before she smiled. "Yes, from the preliminary reports I've read and the report I got from you Friday, I tend to agree with you." She pointed to the portfolio leaning against Becca's chair. "Why did you bring that?"

"Mr. Douglas said I should bring everything I had about Knox to show you."

"Really? What else did he say?"

Becca looked away.

"Look at me," Chase commanded.

Becca lifted her eyes.

"What else did he say?"

"That you asked specifically for me." Becca tried but could not break the eye contact.

"What else?"

Becca thought how best to present her boss's parting remark.

I'm in a catch twenty-two situation. No matter what I say, I lose. She opened her mouth to speak then clamped it shut.

"I am only interested in the truth, Becca." Chase spoke the words softly. "There never will be adverse repercussions from me when I'm told the truth. You have nothing to fear from me, Becca. If it is Mr. Douglas you fear then I *must* know for he is my responsibility."

Becca shook her head and laughed. "I should have stayed in bed."

"Perhaps. I still need to know."

"He said that if I screwed it up and you nixed the project, I wouldn't have a job." Becca watched Chase's face for her reaction. She didn't have long to wait as the woman's eyes pierced her.

"He said that?" Chase's voice dropped an octave.

Becca nodded. She could hear the restrained anger in the voice of the woman sitting next to her. "Do you understand that to remain professional and not be known as a snitch, I should be loyal to my boss no matter the cost? At the same time, I must tell you the truth. Either way I lose."

Chase stood, walked to the window, and stood there with her fists balled. "I can assure you that you will not lose your job by telling me the truth. As for Jim Douglas, I will handle him in my own way." She turned and looked a Becca. "Since you brought the presentation with you, why don't you show me what you have?"

Chase went to her desk and sat in her high-backed leather chair.

✝

Forty-five minutes later, Becca finished the presentation. "Of course this will go faster when we have it all set up instead of me pulling them out to show you."

"Impressive," Chase said. "How much of that is the teams' and how much did Jim contribute?'

Becca shook her head. "I proofed the parts as various members of the team gave them to me. We would have meetings and bounce ideas around then I assembled the presentation and showed it to Mr. Douglas. It was a great team effort."

"And your boss, what did he contribute?"

"He gave the go ahead for the project to be presented to the client."

"You're saying he had little to do with it other than approving what others had done. Is that correct?"

Becca felt her stomach clench from the vitriol in Chase's voice. "That is how it has always been since I've worked for Mr. Douglas. He gives me the details and it is up to me to make sure everything runs smoothly and is on time.

"I see."

Although Chase appeared calm on the outside, Becca saw the outrage in her eyes and the slight coloring to her cheeks. "It works for the team," she added.

"The way I understand this is that the team does all the work and their boss…your boss, Mr. Douglas does nothing. Am I wrong in that supposition?"

"Damn," Becca whispered.

"Why *damn*?"

"You are placing me in another catch twenty-two situation."

Chase stood from her desk and moved toward Becca. "I'm sorry I put you in this situation. The Knox project will go forward and I see no reason for them to reject the proposal. Your job is secure for as long as you want it to be." Chase pursed her lips. "What would you say if I told you there was another PA job opening soon? Would you be interested?"

Becca searched Chase's eyes for any sign of deception and saw none and felt empowered to speak her mind. "Better the devil you know than the one you don't."

"How would you know if you didn't try? Perhaps the new devil is an angel in disguise." Chase looked at her watch then winked. "I'd enjoy spending the day with you trading cryptic remarks unfortunately I have a meeting to attend in five minutes."

Becca didn't know what to say. *Is she coming on to me? No way. Don't be ridiculous.* "Then I will go. Thank you for your time and your kind remarks about the Knox project. Is it okay to tell Mr. Douglas that you approve so he doesn't have to fire me?"

Chase touched Becca's hand. "Think about what I said. If you want a change let me know and I will make it happen."

With averted eyes, Becca began putting her displays back in the valise. "I will."

Once she had everything together, Becca held out her hand. "May I ask you one quick question before I go?"

"Shoot.

Becca mustered all her courage then opened her mouth. "You said there was more than one reason you came to my office this past Friday."

Chase nodded.

"Am I out of line in asking what the other reason, or reasons, was?"

With her arms loose and her hands folded in front of her, Chase looked away before her gaze returned to Becca. "The truth?"

"Yes."

"I was hoping you'd go out to dinner with me."

Becca's eyes grew wide with skepticism. "Really?"

"Yes, really. I've wanted to ask you out for a very long time…it just never worked out time and people wise. I was in the parking lot Friday night and saw your light on so I decided to take a chance with you."

"I'm glad you did. It's been a long time since I've had such a good time."

"Likewise." Chase walked Becca to the door and opened it. "Thank you. Here's my card with my private number on the back. If you give me a call later we can work out when and where our next date will be."

Becca forced her gaze away from Chase's and took in a deep breath. "A date? Like a real date…romantic kind of thing."

Chase laughed. "Yes, that is exactly what I mean. Does it scare you to be asked out by a woman?"

"No, I only date women. I'm just surprised you want to go out with me."

"I can say the same thing about you, Becca." Chase chuckled. "We'll talk later."

Becca walked through the door and heard it click softly shut behind her. When she reached the reception area, she smiled at the woman behind the desk. "Have a good day, Debra," she said heading toward the elevator.

"I don't believe she wants to go out on a date with me," she mumbled while walking to the elevator. When the door closed behind her, she grinned. "She is quite remarkable."

✝

As soon as the elevator doors opened, Douglas was barreling his way toward her. "So, what did she say? Did she scrap the whole thing or just a part?"

Becca waved her folder and grinned. "You won't have to fire me, Mr. Douglas. She was very complimentary of the project and the team."

Jim put his hand over his heart in dramatic fashion that was not becoming of a man in his position. For a moment, Becca thought he might cry.

"Is everything okay?" she asked.

"What a stupid question. Of course, I'm okay now that I know you didn't manage to sabotage the project with Hunter. What else did she say?"

"Not much else really." Becca shook her head. *Selfish bastard he just thinks of himself.*

She walked toward her office. Chase told her that she would always have a job and could have a new boss if she wanted. That knowledge alone empowered her. She did not care for Jim Douglas and never had. He was nothing more than a bully who never showed remorse for any of his actions or words. She actually felt sorry for his family.

Once inside her office, Becca closed the door and waited, anticipating that Jim Douglas barging into her office at any moment to berate her more.

"I should have said *yes* to the offer of a new job. Damn. It was a perfect opportunity to turn things around and I acted like a scatterbrain."

The door didn't open and she sighed in relief.

Her fingers caressed the embossed letters of the card Chase had given her. "This fantastic wonderful woman wants to date me…Becca the PA. How did I get so lucky?"

Chapter Six

Wednesday was a whirlwind of motion as the entire team of six set up the room for Eastman's proposal for the Knox project the next day. Becca stood with her hands on her hips surveying the room. "It looks good, guys. This was a tough one but thanks to all your hard work I'm certain it will be a winner."

"If it hadn't been for your vision, Becca, it never would have happened." Joyce Westcott, blushed before she and other members of the team applauded.

"Thank you. It really was a team effort. I can honestly say that everyone contributed significantly on the project." She cleared her throat. "Now, if you will allow me, I'd like to take you all out to dinner tonight. If you have a significant other they are also invited."

"Is Mr. Douglas coming too," Sam Patterson asked.

"No. No, he isn't."

"Good, then I will attend."

Becca saw the relief on the faces of the team but knew she needed to be professional and say something complimentary about their boss.

"He has other plans." She swallowed hard the lie stuck in her craw. "What about Angelo's." Becca looked at her wristwatch. "Wow, look at the time. Why don't we all make it an early day and leave in maybe forty-five minutes. That will give you time to set things up with whomever you want to invite. I will make the reservations for five-thirty.

That way we can all get home early and be ready for tomorrow."

Everyone nodded and thanked Becca as they left her in the presentation room. She fingered Chase Hunter's card in her pocket and debated whether to call or not.

I'd like to be with her at the dinner. No, it will only cause speculation and I am certain she doesn't want that. It will wait until tomorrow when this is finished and Knox is a done deal.

✝

The watcher, wrapped in a subzero-sleeping bag, kept watch for Becca's headlights and was surprised when they shone at seven-thirty.

Wonder why she's early.

Gwen fortunately left early and that had enabled the watcher to add herbs to the simmering soup on the stove and put a fresh sachet of spice and herbs between the mattress and the box spring. It had taken hundreds of tries at blending the herbs so Becca would find relief from her nightmares. Now that the current mixture seemed to be helpful, the watcher made sure that a fresh sachet was between the mattresses each week.

Becca, if only I could find a cure for the sadness that hovers around you like a shield. Unfortunately, I must wait until you recognize who you are looking for on your own. In that I cannot interfere, the watcher thought, the sentiments like a supplication. *She's there—you just have to see her. You're not a player but sometimes a pretty face makes you turn your head.*

For the next hour, the watcher endured the cold, waiting for Becca to turn out the lights and go to bed. When the familiar sight of Becca standing at the window with her hand on the windowpane came into view, the watcher mimicked the motion.

How I wish I could answer her prayer.

†

Becca woke with a start and in a panic that she'd overslept on this important day. She looked at the bedside clock—she had.

"Shit! Today of all days I have to oversleep." She hadn't checked the clock radio alarm the night before. Gwen sometimes turned it off when listening to music as she cleaned.

In record time, Becca showered, dressed in her best power suit and was on her way to work almost on schedule. She knew that Mr. Douglas would be standing in front of the elevators waiting for her and tapping his foot. Becca lowered her shoulders as all the anxiety she was feeling drained from her. The project was spot on and there was no doubt in her mind that it would go forward as is. She had an ace in her pocket in the form of Chase Hunter.

Once today is finished, I will invite her out for dinner or maybe she can come here and I will cook for her. Becca shook her head and laughed at the thought.

†

"Well, I see you finally decided to show up, Cameron. You know how important this day is and here you come lollygagging in here as if it's nothing. I will not stand for it! Do I make myself clear?"

"Perfectly, sir." Becca looked at the people standing nearby and she knew they were pretending not to hear the verbal abuse. *I've had enough.*

"Good." Douglas growled before walking away.

45

Asshole.

Becca turned and walked away, avoiding the eyes of her team. She knew they were watching her. to refrain from going after her boss and telling him exactly what she thought of him, Becca bit her cheek. Someone touched her shoulder and she stopped abruptly, balled her hand, and turned to whomever it was behind her.

"Oh, Kim. What are you doing here?"

"I came by to tell you good luck on the big presentation." Kim smiled and nodded toward Douglas. "He's a jerk. Don't let him get to you. If you do, he wins and he isn't worth the time of day."

Becca closed her eyes and smiled at her friend. "You're right."

She longed to tell Kim about the meeting with one of the vice presidents but didn't want to jinx anything in case Chase wasn't sincere about dating her.

"I'm thinking seriously about sending my resume out. I've had enough of his shit."

"Wait till you settle down before doing anything rash that might come back to bite you."

"I will. Right now, I need to get the group together and go through the room once more before everyone shows up at nine."

Becca touched Kim's hand. "Thanks for being here for me."

✝

Becca nodded at Chase when she entered the room but her attention turned immediately to her boss who was standing in the front of the presentation room.

Reading from notes that Becca had provided him, he began the presentation for the Knox project. He followed the script exactly thereby making him seem more important than he was.

As he droned on, Becca felt eyes on her and turned her head to see Chase frowning at her.

Does she think I stole my presentation from him? Surely not.

Becca gave the woman a quizzical look and received a wink in return. She felt her face heat up and looked away.

Once Douglas was done with the presentation, Chase spoke. "What is the exact ratio of the profit margin to the cost for Eastman, Jim?"

"Um, well, I don't have those notes with me. I can get them to you once I return to my office."

"Isn't that something that you should know without looking at your notes?"

"Well, yes it is and I do know but for the life of me I cannot recall what that is right now."

"Ms. Cameron, do you know what the ratio is?"

Becca swallowed hard. She saw her boss glaring, daring her to speak. Her eyes then fell on Chase.

"It is five to one."

"Thank you." Chase let a small smile curve her lips.

†

Becca had the team gathered around her after the proposal was accepted.

"I want to thank you all for the long hours and weekends away from your families." From a bag she was carrying, Becca pulled out five envelopes and five gift-wrapped boxes. "I know we didn't get any recognition for what we did but I want you all to know how much I value each of you."

Douglas walked up to the group with a scowl on his face. "What's this?"

Annoyed, Becca ignored the man.

"Are you giving them gifts? I hope my name is on the tags," he said elbowing his way into the group. "You've pulled this before and have always left my name off the gifts."

Becca swiveled around. "You are not part of this. Your name is not on anything just as you failed to mention the team in there." She pointed to the conference room. "All of us who did all the research and made the acquisition happen."

"I insist that you let me pay whatever it cost you. It *is* after all *my* team." Douglas had a snarl on his face as he thumped on his chest. "*My* team, Cameron, *mine* not yours."

Becca turned back to the group that had become silent. "Please accept these as *my* way of saying thank you."

Douglas puffed out his chest. "Don't listen to Cameron here. She doesn't want you to know that I had a hand in those gifts."

Becca spun around. "No, you did not!" Her eyes tracked to the person standing behind her boss.

"Come with me to my office, right now," Douglas demanded.

"Jim, forget your PA. You and I have more important things to discuss. You need to come with me. Now."

"This isn't any of your busi—" Jim turned, "Oh, Ms. Hunter, I didn't know you were there."

"Obviously." Her voice was cold and icy. "Go to your office and I will be there directly."

Chase then turned to the group. "I know how much time all of you put in on this project and I want to personally thank each of you."

Chase moved forward and shook each person's hand, thanking him or her by name before facing Becca. "It was a nice touch that you took them all out to dinner last night and now these gifts. Will you allow the company to compensate you?"

Becca smiled at her team who were murmuring thank you as they dispersed. Once they were gone, she turned back to Chase.

"No. No, it is what I do when my team does an exceptional job."

Chase closed the small conference room's door.

"I know what your salary is. Those crystal key chains aren't cheap." She crooked her head. "How much did you give each of them?"

Becca lowered her head.

"The team doesn't get paid anywhere near what they are worth. I want to give back and in this market, money matters." She winked. "Didn't you know I'm independently wealthy?"

Becca leaned in a bit closer. "I wanted to ask you to join us for dinner last night."

"Why didn't you? I would have liked going."

"You would have accepted my invitation?"

"Of course."

"What about the gossip mongers?"

"There wouldn't have been any for I would insist it was an official company function that required my presence."

"Now I wish I'd called 555-8209 and asked you."

Chase let out a rich melodic laugh. "You've memorized it."

"Of course I did."

"Good to know." Chase held out her hand. "Thank you, Ms. Cameron, for all the hard work you do for Eastman." Chase made sure her voice rose in case her voice carried past the door. "The success of Eastman is only as good as its employees and you and the team are some of the best."

"Thank you, Ms. Hunter." Becca let a smile fill her face.

"No, thank you," Chase whispered. "It is refreshing to know there are selfless people left in the world."

†

Becca saw her boss's office from her desk. Mr. Douglas was standing by the door and Chase was behind his desk.

Nice power move.

Although she could hear the muffled sound of her boss's voice, she did not hear Chase's voice when she spoke. She did however, see Chase slap the desk with her hand.

Chase opened the door and looked in Becca's direction briefly before walking away at a quick pace.

Becca's eyes tracked back to Mr. Douglas's office and she saw him sitting at his desk with his hands covering his face. She watched as his hands lowered and he glared at her. He pushed back from his desk and looked as though he was going to stand but didn't. Instead, he continued to stare at her with what she could only call contempt. He finally got up, went to the door, and slammed it close.

Becca could only speculate as to what Chase had said to the man and what her boss' retaliation toward her would be.

Chapter Seven

Becca knew that it was customary for all the company's executives to gather in the atrium for a celebratory meeting with drinks and hors d'oeuvres after an acquisition. It was up to their immediate bosses if their PA's attended—Mr. Douglas had never invited her.

Just as Becca finished shredding all the miscellaneous Knox papers, a familiar voice spoke.

"Ms. Hunter asked me to give you this."

Chase's receptionist, Debra Kolinsky from the eighteenth floor handed Becca an envelope.

"Thank you." Becca smiled. "Debra, right?"

The woman grinned. "Yes," she said before leaving Becca's office.

"What can this be?" Becca sliced open the envelope and pulled out a hand written note.

Ms. Cameron,
Would you and your team please attend the celebratory gathering in the atrium at four o'clock as my guests?
Regards,
Chase Hunter
VP for Acquisitions

Becca read the note again and shook her head. "Wow." Her phone rang.

"Cameron… Yes, I got one too, Joyce. Gather the others and meet me at the elevators at three-fifty-five. We will all go there together and arrive as a team… I have no idea why she invited us... She probably wanted us recognized for all the work we did… All I know is that Ms. Hunter specifically asked us, therefore we have to attend… I don't know how long we should stay but I'm sure we can leave after being there an hour."

Becca could hear the panic in Joyce's voice.

"Yes, I know you have kids and a husband, Joyce. You can leave the function at five, your normal day's end."

Becca chuckled.

"There's no need for anyone to worry. It is a nice gesture toward us. None of you will have to stay past your regular working hours… I don't know how long I will stay. I do need to get home and let Georgie out… I'll see you all in a little bit, Joyce. Just remember it is all good."

After hanging up the phone, Becca couldn't keep the smile off her face.

"We have a guardian angel looking over the team and her name is Chase Hunter." Becca could feel a tingling along her spine.

✝

The band of six exited the elevator and made their way to the atrium. Becca had the handwritten note from Chase tucked in the side pocket of her suit jacket just in case she needed it. Someone might want confirmation of who they were and why they were there. Becca drew back her shoulders confidently as she led them into the atrium. She scanned the area.

It looks like a who's who of the upper echelon of the company.

She also saw almost all the PA's she knew in attendance. The increasingly familiar feeling of a certain set of eyes focused on her made Becca turn her head to see Chase coming toward her with a smile on her face.

"Good, you all made it. Please come in. I'm happy you accepted my invitation."

"Thank you for inviting us, Ms. Hunter…it was a surprise to all of us." Becca's eyes darted around the room again. "I'm afraid we feel just a bit out of place. We've never been invited to anything like this before."

"Please, there is a table with six chairs there." Chase nodded in the direction of the table. "I'd like you all to sit there."

"You've singled us out? From what I see there are only bistro tables and chairs. Why do we have our own table?" Becca asked.

"Please, go sit at the table and I will answer all your questions shortly."

Becca shrugged. "Okay. Come on, guys, we have special seats."

As she walked, Becca could hear grumblings from her team. She stopped.

"Hey, we're here and it isn't costing us anything so let's just go with the flow and enjoy ourselves."

When she ascertained that everyone nodded, she continued toward the table.

As soon as the team sat down, a waiter appeared and took their drink orders while another of the wait staff placed a plate loaded with hors d'oeuvres on the table.

"What the hell is going on," Sam Peterson whispered. "I've got a bad feeling like this will be our last supper."

Becca scanned the room and found Chase speaking with Edward Eastman the CEO and major stockholder of Eastman. When their eyes met, Chase smiled.

"Don't worry, Sam, I don't think anything nefarious is going to happen."

"Will you look at those hors d'oeuvres," Connie interjected into the conversation. "Wow, this is some kind of rich people's shindig isn't it?"

"And just how do you know that?" Joyce asked Becca.

Becca grinned at Connie's comment then focused on Joyce.

"Because I gave her a private showing of the proposal and I didn't get the feeling she was out to do any of us harm."

"Except for Douglas." Sam chuckled. "I heard that Hunter gave him a proper dressing down this afternoon."

Becca held up her hand.

"Listen, let's just enjoy ourselves and hold back on the gossip. Mr. Douglas is *our* boss and we owe him the respect of that position."

Douglas was standing behind Becca with a scowl on his face.

"What the hell are all of you doing here? You don't belong and I will not have you embarrass me by being party crashers. So get out of here."

Becca pulled the invitation from her pocket and showed it to her boss.

"As you can see we were invited."

"Bitch!" Douglas muttered as he stomped away.

Just as their drinks arrived, the team turned toward the tinkling sound of a knife hitting a glass. Chase was standing behind a small podium and smiled when the room became quiet.

"Thank you all for attending this celebratory gathering. With the merger today of Knox Industries, we are now the biggest telecommunication manufacturing company in the country."

Everyone in the room applauded.

"This never would have happened without the expertise of Jim Douglas' team headed up by Becca Cameron. All too often we, in the top echelons of business, tend to forget at times that there are many who go unrecognized yet do the majority of the work so that we all look successful."

Chase took a drink of water.

"I invited Becca Cameron and the team she leads to join us today so I could publicly recognize them for all the hours they put in to making the Knox plan work." Chase pointed at their table. "Jeff, Sam, Joyce, Connie, Kim, and their team leader Becca, will you all please stand."

Becca scanned the room for Mr. Douglas and saw him glaring at her. Ignoring the look, she grinned at the team.

"Come on guys, this is our moment in the sun."

Applause circled the room then died down.

Chase gripped the podium and spoke loudly. "Thank you all for an outstanding job."

✝

The team stayed for another twenty minutes before one by one they left leaving Becca by herself. She looked around and saw Mr. Douglas. He appeared to be visibly upset, his face red as he pointed his finger at Chase as he spoke with another manager, Clayton Morgan. It was obvious that Clayton was trying to edge away. Becca didn't need to hear what he was saying for she'd heard it all before on more than one occasion. She watched mesmerized by her boss' antics anticipating what would happen if someone like Chase or the CEO overheard him—*they'd probably fire him on the spot.*

Once Clayton Morgan had walked rapidly away, Becca saw her boss looking around the room before he turned and stormed away.

"Hi," Chase said as she sat beside Becca. "I see they all left you behind." A broad smile crossed her face. "Were you pleased?"

"Yes, I was pleasantly surprised. Honestly, since I've been working here no one has ever treated the team so kindly."

"And you?'

Becca found herself lost in Chase's eyes. "You already know the answer to that."

"Yes, I do." Chase held up her glass. "What are you drinking? I'm ready for a refill."

"Just water."

Chase's eyebrows rose. "Water? Are you sure? It is a party after all and the drinks are free."

Becca laughed.

"Remember that my drive home will be very dark since there isn't a moon tonight. It is rutting season so I'll have to be alert."

"What do deer have to do with it?"

"The males run wild with their noses to the ground chasing after the females. They dash across the road and just as you see it, your radiator is smashed in."

"Are you speaking from experience?"

"Yes, I was up close and personal with a young buck. Fortunately, I was driving my truck slow and I came out the winner." Becca grinned. "Bet you never thought of me as a deer slayer."

"Becca, the deer slayer." Chase chuckled. "Never crossed my mind. If you don't mind my asking, why do you live so far away?"

"I live in the house my great-granddaddy built. It's surrounded by two-hundred and fifty acres."

"Don't you get lonely?"

Becca shrugged. "It gets a bit lonely from time to time but I've got George so it isn't so bad."

"Ah, yes. George the dog? So you live alone with your dog. Did you ever live with anyone romantically?"

Becca pursed her lips

"I'm sorry, Becca, I shouldn't have asked you such a personal question."

Chase slid her chair backward and stood.

Becca reached out and held Chase's arm.

"No, please don't go. You didn't ask anything wrong. I was just deciding what to say."

Chase relaxed back into the seat.

"The answer is…there was someone in my life for a short time." She shrugged. "I proved to be a better friend then a lover. She…she just wasn't who I was looking for."

Becca looked directly into Chase's face to judge her reaction. All she saw was a broad grin.

"Don't look now, but, since you are sitting with me, none of our company's players will bother you. Most of the men here are a bit randy and certainly lecherous."

"And you know this from experience?"

"They call me the *ice queen* when they are being kind," Chase shrugged. "I've also heard myself being referred to as *that frigid bitch.*

Becca laughed.

"Because you won't sleep with them or talk to them?" Becca covered her mouth. "Sorry that was a bit too personal."

"Both actually…and I've made it clear that their equipment doesn't interest me."

Becca stared at Chase with her mouth open before she gulped the rest of her water.

"You actually said that to them? Wow."

Chase leaned in closer. "You do know that they are all probably speculating on whether you'll go home with me or not."

"No. Really?"

"Yes, really."

Becca looked around the room and saw heads turn away quickly when she made eye contact.

"But, I'm so far out of your league. Don't they see that?"

"If anyone is out of anybody's league, it's me." Chase touched Becca's arm. "Will you have dinner with me tomorrow night?"

"Um, I am so far out of my comfort zone right now that my head has nothing but empty space," she responded nervously.

Becca looked at her watch.

It's already seven-thirty. I still have to get my things from my office. Damn I won't get home until nine if I'm lucky.

"Do you still have my card?" Chase asked.

Becca nodded.

"Call me tomorrow, okay? Please. I'd really like to get to know you better."

"Okay, I will."

Dazed, Becca watched as Chase got up and walked toward the company's CEO.

Chapter Eight

A cold front made the temperature plummet and the watcher pulled the sleeping bag closer. It was already eight and the watcher's eyes kept a close look on the road. An hour later, the lights from Becca's truck made their way closer to the house.

"Finally, my dear. I was about to freeze to death," the watcher muttered.

The watcher could tell when Becca exited the truck something had happened to her. It was in the way she walked. One minute light and airy the next her feet didn't seem to move. *What has happened to you?* With an earpiece set in one ear, the watcher listened as Becca spoke to George…

"I don't know what to do, girl. It's been a long time since someone has made my heart beat so hard. Do you think I have an answer to my prayers or am I just fooling myself about something that isn't really there?" Becca blew her nose. "God, I miss you so much, Mom. If you were still here, you'd know what I should do. Come on, girl, let's go to bed. I can't remember ever feeling this tired."

With sure steady steps, the watcher made the way down the deer stand's ladder then with a wide smile walked toward the deer path that would lead to home.

"I must come up with a way for Becca to open her heart again. Perhaps that will be easier now that she is getting a good night's sleep."

As the watcher walked, a plan was formulating to bring happiness to Becca. "I won't let you down, my old friend."

✝

Friday morning Becca woke hearing the alarm music and feeling refreshed and relaxed. The project was finished and a success. She didn't have to rush to work even though she knew her boss would be waiting for her to give her a dressing down. She knew he would tell her that the gathering was only for the elite within the company and not for underlings. There was no doubt in Becca's mind that he would expound on how embarrassed she and the team made him and then he would threaten to fire her. She had already told the other team members to take the day off so she knew she was sparing them his wrath.

"I am not going to allow that man to continue to abuse me," Becca said to George when she let her out the door. "Was I dreaming or did Chase Hunter ask me out on a date last night?"

She chuckled. "She did ask me and told me to call her this morning." Becca looked at the wall clock. "I guess seven-fifteen is too early.

Once George had food and water, Becca snagged her breakfast, which consisted of toast and coffee and went outside to her truck. It was a clear crisp morning and the smell of autumn was in the air. No sooner had she reached the flashing light, than her cell rang.

"Damn, I am so not ready to deal with him today." She looked at the display on the screen in the dash and saw a number she did not recognize.

"Cameron." Becca heard a whirring sound. "Hello."

The phone disconnected.

"That was weird. What is it that Kim keeps telling me? Oh, yeah, don't answer if you don't know who it is or it is someone you don't want to talk to."

Becca turned up the radio and disconnected the Bluetooth for her phone. She was already late and decided not to deal with Mr. Douglas until she had to.

"That means not answering it."

†

Becca checked her make-up once more in the rearview mirror before she got out of her vehicle. Her wavy auburn hair insisted on making wild curls on the side of her head and it was driving her crazy.

"I need a haircut…this weekend for sure," she promised herself.

She leaned and picked up the cell phone she had discarded on the passenger seat. When Becca flicked it on and looked at the screen, her eyebrows rose. *Mr. Douglas hasn't called me. That isn't like him.*

A sinking feeling spread through her body. "He's going to fire me, I just know it."

†

Just as the elevator doors closed, the familiar gloved hand of the woman Becca had seen before kept the doors open.

Becca smiled realizing that she had missed the daily ritual during the past week.

I wonder who she is and where she goes after I get off the elevator. There are only two floors above me so one of them has to be it. Perhaps next week I will ride the elevator to the top floor just to see where she goes.

As her floor neared, a knot twisted in Becca's belly in anticipation of seeing her boss's beet red face with his hands on his hips as he waited for the elevator door to open. Becca sucked in a deep breath. When the doors slid open—Mr. Douglas was standing there just as she expected. His face flushed and the veins on his neck stood out in bas-relief.

Oh, this is bad. He's going to fire me. I just know it. Good thing I have an ace up my sleeve.

"Well, look who finally decided to come to work. I guess you think that the Hunter woman is going to protect you. You're wrong, Cameron." His eyes bored into her. "I am the boss around here and if you ever embarrass me again like you did last night you will be very sorry. That is a promise."

Becca swallowed hard. "Are you threatening me, Mr. Douglas?"

"Like I said…it is a promise and not a threat." He turned and stomped off toward his office.

Becca was shaking so violently that she had to lean against a wall to steady her body.

"Are you okay?" Connie Bollinger, one of her team members asked. "Becca?"

The sound of a gentle voice finally reached Becca and she looked for the source. "Oh, Connie, I didn't see you there."

Without saying a word, Connie wrapped her hand around Becca's arm and walked her toward Connie's cubicle.

"Sit and I will get you some water."

Becca's eyes focused on her surroundings and willed her body to stop quivering. For the moment, she was safe hiding from her boss's fury but knew she couldn't stay there forever. Eventually she'd have to go to her office and face the man who would be sitting in full view in the office across from her.

"Here you go," Connie handed Becca a plastic cup filled with water. "Drink some of that water then take a few deep breaths to calm down."

Becca looked up at Connie with a weak smile. "Thanks, Connie, I…I don't know what happened. Not enough sleep, I guess."

Connie took a seat next to Becca, and took her hand. "I heard everything he said as did everyone within hearing range. If you'd like me to, I can fill out a complaint form. You can sign it, and then I will take it to HR personally."

Becca shook her head. "Right now I'm too terrified to take any action. You didn't see the rage in his eyes. I do believe he will physically hurt me if I do anything."

"I've worked with you for almost three years, Becca, and the last thing I expected from you is a coward." She squeezed Becca's hand. "You cannot let him get away with this. If you won't fill out a complaint, maybe you can speak with Ms. Hunter. She seems like a really nice person."

"Maybe I will do that. Thanks, Connie." Becca could still feel her body trembling deep inside. "Do you think you would walk with me to my office and stay there with me for a little bit?"

A warm smile was on Connie's face. "Of course I will and I'll stay as long as you want me to."

Becca's eyebrow rose. "Hey, why are you here? I thought I told you all to take the day off."

"Yes, you did." Connie shrugged. "After yesterday and his reaction to our being there I wanted to make sure you were okay."

✝

Becca and Connie walked to her office. The whole time Becca was glancing over her shoulder wondering if Mr. Douglas was anywhere in sight. She let out a sigh of relief when she saw that her boss's door was closed.

"Good his door is closed," Becca whispered. "Once I get inside my office and get the door closed I will be safe for the time being."

"Are you sure?" Connie asked in an equally soft voice. "I can stay as long as you want me to."

"I'll be okay. I will lock the door so he can't barge in."

With a shaking hand, Becca unlocked her door before turning to Connie. "Thank you so much for coming to my rescue. I will be okay now."

"You're sure?"

"Yes. Since you're here, will you please shred all the old Knox information for me? Then go home and enjoy some time off. You've earned it."

"Not a problem." Connie turned to go back to her office when she looked back at Becca. "Is it okay if I call you later to see how you're doing?"

"Yes, I'd like that." Becca watched as Connie walked away before opening her office door and going inside.

✝

Becca casually glanced at her desk then took a second look. A crystal bud vase with a single red rose was sitting in the middle of her desk. Becca smiled and moved into her office, hung up her coat, placed her briefcase on the desk, locked the door, and sat in her chair. Becca stared at the rose and it occurred to her that she hoped Chase had sent it to her. If it were an *I'm sorry* from her boss, he would have given her a gift certificate to a restaurant just as he did at holiday time.

A piece of folded pink paper in the shape of a heart was on the desk next to the vase and Becca picked it up and unfolded it.

Becca, I can't believe how responsive your body was to my touch. I loved waking up next to you and taking you again. Love, C.

"What kind of sick joke is this?" She reread the note, picked up the phone, and tapped in the number that was on the back of Chase's card. She pressed the speakerphone button.

"Hunter."

The soft melodic sound of Chase's voice filled Becca's ears and made her anger dissipate. "Hi, it's Becca."

"Becca, hi. This is a pleasant surprise."

The soft tenderness in Chase's voice was unmistakable to Becca. "Is there a good time for you to come to my office today?"

"I'll make time. What's this about?"

It felt like the lump in her throat wouldn't let her speak, and Becca closed her eyes willing the trembling she was feeling to stop.

"Becca, I'll be right there."

For several seconds Becca held on to the phone as if it were a lifeline.

I just need to keep it together until Chase gets here.

It seemed as though Chase was knocking on her door as she hung up. She couldn't have gotten here that fast. Becca was shaking as she moved to the door, peeked through the blind and saw it was indeed Chase. Her shoulders relaxed. She unlocked the door and opened it.

"I'm so glad to see you."

Chase entered Becca's office. "Why did you have your door locked? What's happened?"

"Please close the door and lock it," Becca whispered.

Mr. Douglas was sitting at his desk glaring at her.

At this moment, I don't give a flying crap what he thinks, she thought. When the door shut and she heard the lock click into place, Becca let out a sigh of relief.

"Okay, now tell me please what's going on. I can see your body shaking. Please what's happened?"

"When I came into my office this morning," Becca said as she pointed to her desk. "That was there along with this note." Becca held up the heart shaped pink note. "I'm pretty sure you did not send it to me."

Becca reached across her desk and offered Chase the note.

Chase opened the folded heart, read the contents, turned toward the door, and glared toward Douglas' office.

"It's a good thing the blinds are shut," Chase growled. "Did he do this?"

Becca shook her head. "I can't see him having the balls to do something so blatant."

"Come with me." Chase stood by the door waiting for Becca before she opened it.

†

The two women exited the office and Becca locked the door before they headed for the elevators.

Jim Douglas' door opened wide. "Where do you think you're going, Cameron? Get back in your office until *I* tell you it is time to leave."

Chase squeezed Becca's shoulder gently. "Keep walking and I'll meet you at the elevators." Chase turned and walked back to the red-faced man. When she was standing toe to toe with Douglas, Chase narrowed her eyes. "You will go back in your office and stay there."

"I want that bitch of a PA I am stuck with to come back now!"

"Jim," Chase's voice dropped an octave. "If you're smart, you will stop this and go back into your office."

"The hell I will. That lying bitch is telling you stories that have no basis in fact. She needs to be fired."

"You may not speak in a derogatory manner about any employee of Eastman. I *am* your boss and *I* am telling you to back off." Chase's eyes were blazing with anger.

Douglas turned to his office. "Dyke bitch," he mumbled.

"Stop right there, Mr. Douglas." Chase watched as the man turned around. "If you want to keep your job, you will not speak to me in that manner either. In case you've forgotten, I am the one who has a hand in the hiring and firing. I am your direct supervisor and I suggest you show me the proper respect or *you will* find yourself without a job."

"You can't do that." Douglas sneered. "Eastman won't allow you to fire me. You have nothing to merit firing me."

"That, Jim, is where you are wrong." Chase balled her hands into fists. "I suggest you go into your office, shut the door, and wait for me to return."

She turned and walked away, hearing a door slam behind her.

✝

When Chase caught up with Becca at the elevators, she smiled.

"Did he fire me?" Becca closed her eyes.

"That isn't his option. It is mine and as I told you, you will always have a job at Eastman." Chase gently squeezed

Becca's shoulder again before she pressed the elevator down button.

"What now?" Becca bowed her head.

"Now, we are going to go down to security on the second floor and watch the footage of your floor from this past evening until you arrived at your office this morning."

"And find out who sent that message and flower."

Chase could tell the note had disturbed Becca. She let out a quiet snort. *I'm disturbed, too.*

The doors slid open and both Becca and Chase entered the empty elevator.

Chase entered her keycard into the slot at the bottom of the button panel and the lights flashed. She turned, pulled Becca into a warm embrace, and could feel her body trembling.

"I will find out who sent that note and I will deal with Douglas."

After the welcome snuggling, Becca stepped back with a slight smile curving her lips. "I don't understand."

"Neither do I, Becca, on both issues. We will find out who is behind the note and flower and he or she will be out of a job by the end of today."

Chase pulled out her override key and pressed the second floor button.

✝

The elevator doors opened and Chase exited followed by Becca.

A genial looking man, wearing glasses and with a full head of black hair sat behind a desk opposite the elevators. "Good morning. Ms. Hunter, it's been a while since we've seen you down here on the second floor. What can we do for you today?"

"It's good to see you too, Charlie. You're right, I don't get down this way much. I need to see the films for the sixteenth floor from last night at six-thirty to this morning at…" Chase turned her attention to Becca.

"Eight should be good," Becca whispered.

"This morning at eight."

"That's an easy enough request. Do you want all angles or just a particular one?"

"The one that goes toward Jim Douglas' office."

"You got it. Do you want to wait or should I send it up to your office?"

"I'll wait. I'd appreciate you putting a rush on my request."

"Let me call back and tell them what you need. After the video is found I will let you view it in one of the vacant offices."

"Great. Which office? We'll wait there."

"Second one on the left."

"Thank you, Charlie."

†

Becca and Chase sat in the empty office, each seemingly lost in their own thoughts.

"Who do you think did this?" Becca asked

"Obviously it is someone who was at the function last night." Chase smiled at Becca and pulled her into another hug. "I'm so sorry for bringing this on you."

"You didn't bring anything on me. It was the creep who sent that rose and the note."

No matter what Becca's words were, Chase could feel the tension radiating from her body. It was palpable and filled every corner of the room. She looked at the phone, willing it to ring. Instead, there was a soft knock on the door.

"Come in."

Charlie poked his head inside the room. "If you turn on the computer and then log in with your password, Ms. Hunter, on the desk top you will see your name and when you click on it you will be able to go through the video of last night through this morning."

"Thank you. I owe you one for making this happen as fast as you did." Chase gave the man an honest smile.

"Weren't nothin' I did." Charlie pointed his thumb over his shoulder. "It was the geeks." He grinned. "Stay in here as long as you need."

"Thanks."

Chase turned on the computer and immediately saw the log in screen. She rapidly entered her password and waited for the screen to refresh.

"Grab a chair and sit next to me," she told Becca.

Becca grabbed the nearest chair and moved so she was sitting next to Chase. For the first time since arriving at work, her shoulders relaxed. She noticed the subtle smell of Chase's perfume. It was the first thing she noticed about Chase when they'd met that first time. Becca watched as Chase's finger tapped the mouse and the program opened.

"Most of this will be boring with no action. I think we won't find anything until later in the evening when the cleaning crew starts working."

"Why then?"

"You locked your door when you left last night…right."

"Yes, I always do." Becca's eyes widened. "I see what you're getting at. Whoever did this must have had a way to get into my office."

"Exactly."

With both their heads almost touching, Becca and Chase watched the video that showed two separate screens. One showed the comings and goings on the elevators and the other along the hallway to Becca's office. The cleaning crew made their way toward Becca's office and Chase slowed down the speed.

Finally, they watched as a man with a single rose in a budvase got off the elevator about four-ten that morning. They saw as he stopped to speak with one of the members of the cleaning crew. He was gesturing toward Becca's office with a grin on his face.

"He's probably telling them some sort of story about an anniversary or birthday and he wants to surprise his girlfriend when she gets to work."

They continued to watch as the man handed what he was carrying to one of the cleaning crew who disappeared back into Becca's office. The pink heart note was evident.

"Do you know who it is?" Becca asked.

Chase nodded. "Yes, and to be honest I'm not surprised."

Becca could hear the anger and disappointment in Chase's voice.

"What are you going to do?"

"Fire him."

The finality and coldness of Chase's voice startled Becca.

"Just like that?"

"Yes, just like that." Chase snapped her fingers. "What he's done is a clear violation of Eastman's zero tolerance policy for sexual harassment." She sighed. "There have been complaints about him in the past but we've never had enough proof to dismiss him. Now we do and he will be out of a job in about an hour."

Chase pressed an intercom button. "Charlie, can you have the techies send that file to my computer for my eyes only?"

"Will do, Ms. Hunter."

"Thank you. The fact that someone got into my office made me feel vulnerable and no longer safe." Becca wrapped her arms around her body.

"Please come to my office around noon and bring your lunch. By then I will have this all sorted out and can update you."

Becca nodded as they both stood and walked to the door.

Chase gave Becca one more hug then opened the door and they made their way to the elevators. When the elevator door opened, Chase pressed the sixteenth and eighteenth floor buttons.

"Don't engage your boss in any way. Just go to your office, go in, and lock the door behind you. I will deal with him. Once I get to my office, I will notify him that for the time being you and the team will report directly to me and no one else."

"Thank you."

Chase's words were appreciated but Becca knew that she would still have to face him the minute she tried to open her door. Becca heard the ding for her floor and felt the familiar knot in her stomach that she now realized haunted her whenever her boss' name floated into her brain.

Chase touched Becca's hand. "Be strong and trust me to protect you," she said softly.

"I do."

Becca smiled, stepped out of the elevator, and fought the anxiety that threatened to overtake her.

Chapter Nine

Becca stood in front of her office door as her trembling hand tried to slip the keycard into the lock. When the card finally slid in and the lock started to disengage, she heard the familiar click of the door behind her. She pulled her keycard out quickly and opened the door but she wasn't quick enough.

"Not so fast there, Cameron."

Mr. Douglas' voice sent a chill of fear up her spine. She did as Chase directed and opened her door, walked inside, and shut the door. A meaty hand on her door stopped her.

"Never would I have pegged you as queer, Cameron, but now I can see clearly that you're a lesbo dyke. How else can you explain the sudden interest in you from that bitch of a VP?"

"Let go of my door, Mr. Douglas, or I *will* call HR about your intimidation tactics and cruel slurs."

"If that is how you want to play it then okay. You're fired immediately. Get your things together, turn in your badge, and get out of this building. I'll give you one hour." He let go of the door.

Becca immediately locked the door and let out the breath she'd been holding. Through the window, she saw her boss on the phone, knowing he was putting her firing into motion. When she saw him stand up and slam the phone down, she smiled.

Chase came through for me.

†

"Rick, this is Hunter."

"What can I do for you, Ms. Hunter.

"What I want to know is *why*?"

"You're going to have to give me more information before I can answer that question."

Chase felt her anger rise and tamped it down. "You know exactly what I mean. Did you think I couldn't figure it out? We do have the building monitored twenty-four-seven."

"I still have no idea what you want, Ms. Hunter."

"Stop with your BS. Do you realize that this little prank of yours has jeopardized your job?"

"A practical joke will get me fired? I doubt it."

"You can't be that stupid. I have your record and I know that you attended all the mandatory human resource meetings. This company takes sexual harassment seriously."

"Aw, come on now. Sexual harassment, you've got to be kidding."

"I assure you, Mr. Ross, I am not kidding. Sending a flower with a romantic note implicating me and another employee having a sexual tryst is not some silly practical joke. It casts disparagements and shows disrespect for all the women that work here at Eastman."

"You have no proof."

"Ah, but I do, Mr. Ross." Chase gnashed her teeth. "You've picked on the wrong woman to take on. As I said, the building is monitored twenty-four-seven. It wasn't hard to locate you speaking to the cleaning crew and having them put the flower and note on her desk. I've contacted the person you spoke to and she told me you said you wanted to surprise your girlfriend."

"Give me a break. You can have all the proof you want. Ed Eastman is a golfing buddy of mine and he isn't going to let you fire one of his best managers."

"Now, you must be kidding. Do you think I just called you up on a whim without speaking with Mr. Eastman first?"

"You fuckin' dyke. I won't let you get away with this. You can count on it. So you'd better back away and leave me alone."

"I don't think you understand, Mr. Ross. You're the manager and I'm the vice president…your direct boss…so you have no say in this matter. Either I see your resignation on my desk in thirty minutes or I will kick this to human resources and you will never find a job again."

"Bitch. You can't do that to me."

"I've heard enough from you, Ross," Edward Eastman said. "As Ms. Hunter said, you have thirty minutes to tender your resignation. After that, there will be no severance pay. We have a folder with complaints about you from several Eastman female employees. HR warned you twice at my behest and you were told then what would happen next."

"Come on, Ed, you can't do this to me. We're buddies."

"I'll leave the rest up to you, Chase," Eastman said and disconnected his line.

"What will you be doing, Mr. Ross? Either way you are fired."

"I will be in your office in thirty minutes," Rick Ross said finally.

"I'm glad you see it my way, Mr. Ross. I will tell Debra to expect you.

Chase slammed the phone down. "Asshole, I should have just given him to the wolves. They hate sexual harassment."

She picked up the receiver once again. "Debra, I am expecting Rick Ross in about a half hour. Will you please escort him to my office then call security?"

†

At noon, Becca picked up her lunch of a turkey wrap and an apple and headed for her office door. She unlocked the door with trepidation and was relieved when Mr. Douglas didn't open his door and harangue her again.

Riding the elevator up two floors, Becca felt butterflies fluttering in her stomach. She knew they weren't from anxiety but from the anticipation of seeing Chase again. When she stepped out of the elevator, she saw Debra just getting up from her desk.

"You can go on back to Ms. Hunter's office," Debra said.

Becca began walking toward Chase's door when she spied the woman who always stuck her hand in each morning, stopping the elevator door from closing. She was sitting in the waiting area eating what looked like a roast beef sandwich. Becca stopped her forward motion and turned back to Debra.

"Who is that woman?" she whispered.

Debra looked at the waiting area. "Oh, that's Doris. She comes by every day and we give her something to eat. Ms. Hunter calls her our *project in restoration*. We look out for her."

"How does she get past security?"

"Oh, Ms. Hunter takes care of that."

†

Becca nodded and walked quickly to Chase's office where she knocked on the door. The door opened almost

76

immediately and Becca found herself drowning in Chase's eyes.

Chase stepped back from the door and smiled. "Come in."

"Thanks. I'm sorry I've caused you so much trouble today. I'm sure you have other more pressing problems than that of a mean spirited joke."

"Nothing to be sorry for, Becca. The truth is, I *did* want to see you today and I had just entered my office when you called." She smiled at Becca and nodded toward the lunch bag. "I see you brought your lunch."

"Yes. I have plenty if you don't mind sharing." Becca, suddenly feeling foolish for bringing her lunch, blushed. "I thought that was what you wanted me to do."

Chase grinned. "I did. I'm just waiting for my lunch to arrive. I did order extra so we can both share."

"I'd like that." Becca looked past Chase to the window and saw dark bluish clouds. "Looks like we might get snow."

Chase turned and saw the darkening sky. "Could be. Come, take a seat and we can chat while we wait."

Becca sat in the same chair she had the week before. *Has it only been a week?* "Will you tell me about Doris?"

Chase's grin was so broad that deep dimples appeared on her cheeks. "Doris is my work in progress." Her eyes brightened. "About three years ago I came to work very early…around five, I think. Doris was propped up against the building and I thought she was dead. When I touched the pulse in her neck, her eyes opened wide."

"You must have freaked her out."

Becca was breathless waiting for Chase to tell her more. Deep down what she really wanted, was to hear the timber of Chase's voice, which she found so alluring.

"My dad has diabetes and I remembered how sweet his breath always was. I smelled the same thing from Doris and brought her inside and had her sit in my office while I hunted up something that was good for her to eat."

"Then what happened?'

"I called a friend of mine who volunteers in a homeless shelter and soup kitchen. She put me in contact with the right agencies to get Doris a medical checkup along with a place to sleep." Chase shrugged. "She comes by most days for either breakfast or lunch. I try to make sure she is safe and has food to eat."

"That's so commendable, Chase. You should get a medal or tell the story to the newspapers and television stations. It's a feel good type of story."

"That's not why I do it. Debra and the guards at the doors are the only ones who know about her connection to me. Doris is a lovely lady and deserves more than life is giving her at this moment."

"Like what?"

"I asked her once how she came to be homeless and she told me she wasn't homeless for the world was her home. She also said she was on a mission but I haven't a clue as to what she meant by that."

There was a soft knock on the door before it opened and Debra came into the room.

"Here's your lunch." She looked at Becca and smiled. "I see you have your own."

Becca nodded. "Yes, I do."

Debra was about to leave when Chase spoke.

"Is Doris still out there?"

"When I left she was."

"Good." Chase scraped the cake off her plate into a small paper plate she'd taken out of her desk. "Give this to her and tell her that it is sugar free."

"Will do." Debra smiled, took the plate, and left the room.

"You order sugar free deserts?" Becca asked, opening her lunch bag.

"Yeah, every day. Just in case Doris comes here for lunch. When she doesn't, we keep it wrapped up for her to have with breakfast."

Becca just stared at Chase enchanted by the woman and her tender soul. "In a way I'm glad I got that rose and note."

"Really? I find that hard to believe."

"If it hadn't happened, then I wouldn't get to see this side of you." Becca grinned for the first time that day—it felt good.

Chase's eyes narrowed. "You should know that the person responsible for the flower and note is no longer working at Eastman."

"Just like that and he's gone? Isn't there some sort of review board that he can appeal to?" Becca shivered as she recalled Mr. Douglas snapping his fingers and saying *just like that*.

"When the major stock holder and CEO of Eastman makes the decision, there is no longer anyone to appeal to."

Becca took a small bite of her turkey wrap before looking directly at Chase who had yet to touch her lunch.

If I tell her about Mr. Douglas then the word will get around that I'm a snitch, especially after someone gets the boot on my account.

She lowered her eyes.

Chase cleared her throat and pushed the plate away. "Becca, I need you to tell me about the way Jim Douglas has treated you during the years."

Becca chewed on her lower lip and looked away. "There's nothing to tell really. He lets me do my job and run the team."

Chase stood and growled. "I don't care where someone comes from or what their job is. Everyone deserves respect and recognition for what they do. It is plain to me that Douglas is bent on taking all the glory for himself."

Her anger made the veins in her forehead stand out. "After his presentation yesterday I consulted with the CEO about his deplorable actions toward his team, who worked nonstop so he'd look good."

"Thank you for watching out for the team. It meant a lot to them that you would single them out and praise them the way you did yesterday. You made them all feel proud for what they had accomplished."

Chase blushed. "Thanks. I'm not sure I'm worthy of your praise. I too have had my moments when I was less than kind." Chase's face turned serious. "Just today, with my own ears, I heard how he talks to you. I don't think it was a one-time incident, Becca. Please tell me about his treatment of you and the team."

For several minutes, Becca warred with herself about what to say. "He is a nasty, mean, foul mouthed man who doesn't do a lick of work if he can help it. His bottom line is to make sure that the team shows him in a favorable light. He accomplishes that through bullying and threatening to fire everyone."

"Why do you stay?" Chase asked in a whisper.

"I can't abandon the team."

"You take all the hits for them?"

"I try to insulate them from his rants. Yes."

"You should know that he called HR and demanded that they start your exit paperwork."

"I didn't know who he called but he did tell me I was fired and to have my things out of the office by the end of the day."

"HR called me to verify that he…."

The phone rang.

"Hunter."

Becca watched as Chase listened intently to whoever was speaking to her.

"Okay, give me five minutes and I'll be there." Chase's face became apologetic. "I have a fire I need to put out." She sighed. "I'm sorry."

Becca smiled. "It's your job so there is nothing to be sorry for. Would you like to come out to my place tomorrow for dinner? We can grill some fish." She saw Chase cringe. "Or not."

"I'd like that very much but fish not so much."

"Okay, steak then."

"Much better. Will you email me the directions?"

Becca nodded.

"And what should I bring?"

"Yourself and an appetite."

Chase walked with Becca to the door. Becca was close enough to feel the energy radiating off Chase. "Why don't you come out early and I can show you around the property."

"I will call you when I leave. Please make sure your cell number is with the directions. I'd hate to show up and find out you are still sleeping." Chase opened the door.

Becca grinned as she passed by her new friend. "See you tomorrow."

"Yes, you will."

✝

Once she shut the door, Chase leaned her back against it. "What's come over me? After three years I finally meet her and now I'm mooning about her like an adolescent," she said softly.

She smiled. *She is cute and under that suit I bet her body is next to perfect,* she thought.

81

Chase pushed away from the door, walked to her desk, sat in her seat, and swiveled around. She looked out the windows that surrounded the corner of her office.

I wish I were the one who sent her the flower. I see so much pain in her eyes that it makes me want to be the one to take it all away.

"Pull yourself together and stop being ridiculous. You know nothing about her sexual life. For all you know she could be a womanizer," she told herself.

In her heart, Chase knew that was far from the truth. Becca was someone special that needed someone in her life other than her dog. *Could that be me?* Chase shook her head. "No. I'll see what happens tomorrow before I decide to move in."

She laughed then sobered as her pager went off. "Right, the fire."

†

Chase was sitting in HR waiting for them to let her into the conference room. She thought back to earlier in the day when she had punched in the number, added Edward Eastman to the conference call, and pressed the speaker button on her phone.Now she was waiting for the obligatory meeting with HR about Rick Ross' termination.

When the door opened and a young man indicated she should enter the room, Chase was not in the best of moods.

"Please, Ms. Hunter, take a seat."

Chase looked at the man in charge of HR. Angus Blackthorn was in his fifties and had been with HR for the past twenty-five years. He was kind and Chase had always gotten along with him but she had a feeling that wouldn't be the case today. She sat and looked around the table at the five people sitting there.

"Would you like some water or something else to drink?" Blackthorn asked in a genial manner.

"No." Chase was holding her anger in check. "I want to know why you have requested that I be here. I've provided you with all the proof you need, along with Mr. Eastman's approval of Ross' termination. Why are you dragging me away from my job when Mr. Ross' actions are so blatant?"

"We have to, Ms. Hunter. Rick Ross filed a complaint against you."

Chase laughed. "You're kidding me right?"

"We have to take every complaint seriously," Angus Blackthorn said. "Rick Ross indicated in his complaint that you set him up because you had someone—who you are romantically involved with—to step in and take his job."

Chase stood. "I am not romantically involved with anyone at the moment and even if I were, I certainly would not risk everything I've worked for. If you look at the video, it is clear what Ross did. I had every right to fire him and, as I said, it was with Mr. Eastman's blessing. This is nothing more than a witch hunt and I will not stay here one more moment listening to this drivel."

She grabbed the back of her chair, slid it back to where it was, and started for the door.

"Ms. Hunter, will you please sit back down." Angus said.

Chase turned and looked everyone in the eye ending with Angus Blackthorn. "No." She left the room.

Outside the door, she pulled out her cell phone and dialed Edward Eastman's private line. "Hello, Edward, I hope I'm not disturbing you… I just wanted to find out if you knew that Ross filed a claim with HR against me… I didn't think so…no, I was summoned to a meeting with Angus and his crowd… of course I am annoyed wouldn't you be? Okay, thank you."

Edward Eastman was going to put a stop to the ridiculous witch-hunt and that was all Chase needed to know.

†

Becca sat at her desk smiling. The rose was no longer on her desk, having found its way to the trash bin. She moved her mouse and the computer screen came to life. Once she had added a map to the directions to her home she was about to press send but stopped. Picking up her phone, she texted a message to the number Chase gave her.

Do you want me to send the directions to this work email or is there another you'd like me to use. She pushed send and waited for a response. After forty minutes, Becca realized that Chase was unavailable and put the composed email in the drafts folder.

For the next hour, Becca sorted through all the documents that had to do with Knox. She placed them in a plastic bin and marked it Knox before placing a seal around the box and adding her initials to the seal. Just as she was about to pick up the phone to call for a pick-up of the box, the phone rang.

"This is Becca Cameron, how may I help you?" Becca said into the hands free speaker.

"You can start by giving Debra the directions when she stops by your office in a few minutes."

Becca could hear the playful smile she was sure was on Chase's face.

With a few quick keystrokes, she opened the draft and printed it out. "And here she is now."

Chase laughed and Becca joined in.

"Will you give me a second?"

"Of course.

Becca moved to the door. "Hi, Debra, give me a minute to put this in an envelope." Becca licked the envelope and wrote Chase Hunter on the front. "Here you go. Thanks."

"You're welcome." Debra looked at the envelope then at Becca. "You must be magic," she shrugged. "I'd better get going."

Becca shook her head as she watched Debra leave.

Magic? Where'd that come from? "Okay the directions are on the way to you now.

"Excellent. I want you to know how much I am looking forward to seeing you and your home tomorrow."

For a long moment, Becca remained silent. "You sure know how to turn a girl's head, Ms. Hunter."

"Oh, do I now?"

Becca laughed. "Like you don't know."

"Hey, didn't I hear Debra say you were magic?"

Becca felt a laugh bubbling up and allowed it to happen. "No idea why she said that. I thought it was a rather bizarre thing for her to say."

"Want me to tell you a secret?" Chase chuckled. "It will answer the magic question."

"Please do."

"Hmm, perhaps I should save it for tomorrow."

"Hey, not fair. Please tell me."

"Well, since you asked so nicely, I will tell you now." Chase cleared her throat. "Umm I've worked with Debra for five years now and from the start, she was always trying to hook me up with one guy or another. So, I had to tell her that I wasn't interested in guys but girls."

Chase laughed. "After that it has been a slew of women's names from her. Some I went out with once but most I passed on. I guess my smiles have given me away when she asked if I was interested in you. I, of course, said *yes* and her answer was *she must have put some kind of spell on you.*"

Becca laughed. "Oh no, I've been outed as a spell caster. Darn, I was hoping to keep that a secret." She giggled. "Does that mean that if I'm interested in you, that you cast a spell on me?"

"Interesting topic. We will have to discuss it at length tomorrow. By the way, I was wondering what time breakfast was since you did say come early."

Becca laughed. "Breakfast will be served when you arrive. Did I tell you I have chickens and you can have the freshest egg you'll ever have?"

"Yum, can't wait. Are you finished for the day?"

"Yes, I just finished the cataloging of all the Knox files and once I call for a pickup I'll be done."

"I understand you told the team to take today off."

"It is the least I could do for them after all the missed football games and birthday parties."

"So why did you come in today?"

"Um." Becca stalled trying to come up with a reason for her not taking the day off too. "Well, I wasn't hoping for a rose in a bud vase I can tell you that."

"Right. Now tell me the real reason."

"Truthfully, if I didn't come into the office Mr. Douglas would have been on the warpath and I was hoping to…"

"To what, Becca."

"See you." Becca could hear the intake of a breath and her heart sank. *I should have kept my mouth shut.* "I guess I will go now."

"Home?"

"No, it's not time yet."

"Yes, it is. Go home and rest up. I hear you have a visitor coming very early in the morning." Chase laughed.

"And I understand she is very hungry for eggs fresh from a chicken's ass."

There was silence until Becca heard. "Thanks, Debra."

"Do you want to take a minute to look at the directions in case you have any questions?"

"No, the GPS on my car always seems to get me to where I'm going. Please go home, Becca, and don't worry about Douglas coming down on you. Remember you now report to me only."

"What about the team? He'll just find someone else to pick on."

"Trust me. The team is safe too."

"I do," Becca whispered. "Thank you, I'll see you in the morning."

"Count on it."

Chapter Ten

On the way home, Becca stopped at a large supermarket to pick up groceries for the next day. She spent a long time picking out only the freshest and ripest fruits and vegetables available. It wasn't often she cooked for anyone other than herself and Georgie but she knew could still put a decent meal together. She smiled recalling Chase asking about breakfast.

Wonder if she will be early enough for breakfast.

She wheeled her cart around until she found the bacon rationalizing that everybody likes bacon. The feeling of butterflies fluttering around in her stomach every time she thought of Chase made Becca smile. Buying food that she knew Chase would eat only made the butterfly's wings flap harder.

Becca was driving along a boring straight road with nothing of interest on either side listening to the radio and singing along. She heard her phone ring and engaged the Bluetooth. "Hello."

Static echoed in her ear.

"Hello, is anyone there."

Static. She waited for the phone to ring again but it didn't. "That's just weird."

In the distance she spied the overpass and knew she'd be home in a matter of ten minutes.

✝

The watcher took advantage of the mild temperatures to enter Becca's home and plant another listening device in the kitchen. The sound of a vehicle's door slamming shut made the watcher stop and frown before taking a quick look out the window.

Becca was home early.

From watching Becca daily, the watcher knew that that Becca was a creature of habit and came and went close to the same time every day. A fact that made it easy leaving the house undetected. Not today. Georgie was sitting at the front door with a waging stub of a tail waiting for her mistress to open the door.

With stealth, the watcher opened the back door and left the house just as Becca placed a key in the lock.

Now for the tricky part—getting to the cover of the trees without Becca seeing me.

With quick steps, the watcher crossed the walled back yard and made it behind the chicken coop just as the screen door opened and the dog came bounding out of the house running toward the coop.

"Georgette, you get back here and leave those chickens alone. If you get them all riled up they won't lay eggs and I need them."

The watcher stood stock still as Becca came toward the hen house. *She can't see me.* With silent steps, the watcher made it to the gate and opened it, hoping it wouldn't make a sound. It was the watcher's great fortune that Georgie was barking as the gate swung open with a creak then closed.

Forced to take the long way around, the watcher finally made it back to the deer stand and climbed the ladder. Once settled, the watcher placed a small listening device in the right ear.

"Is she crying?"

Grabbing binoculars and focusing on the window in the kitchen, the watcher saw Becca sitting with her elbows on the table and her face buried in her hands.

"God, what the hell am I doing?" The watcher heard Becca sob. "I can't do this. I can't let a stranger be here. It's bad enough when Kim visits. At least she knows about how callous and unfeeling I was, and that I was the cause of the accident and the death. Why couldn't I just have replaced the damn light bulb?

The watcher listened to the pain encrusted words and wished there was some way to trade places with Becca so she could see what a wonderful woman she was.

Accident's just happen, sweetheart. They are unintended and happen no matter how careful you are.

The watcher concentrated hard, hoping that Becca would hear the words. That was all that the watcher could do. The rules were very specific—no direct contact.

†

By the time Becca pushed away from the kitchen table, it was getting dark. She thought she had locked all the past away and it would have stayed there had she not invited Chase to her home.

It's the place where everyone I love dies.

With a shake of her head, she squeezed her eyes tight. "I should call her and tell her not to come."

Just then, the phone rang. Becca pressed the speaker button. "Hello," she said in a shaky voice.

"Becca, what's the matter?"

"Hi, Kim."

"I looked for you today…are you sick?"

Becca ran the back of her hand across her nose. "No. No, I'm not sick. Just a bit melancholy, that's all."

"Want me to come out?"

"Thanks, but *no*. I'll be okay."

"Any idea what brought it on?"

Becca nodded.

"Bec?"

"Yeah, I met someone and I invited her to come out here tomorrow."

"Oh? That shouldn't be something to feel blue about."

Becca ignored the hollow reply. "Can you believe that we only met a week and a half ago and I've already asked her to come out here?"

"She must be someone very special. You don't usually let your heart get that close to anyone. Maybe it's a good sign, Bec. Maybe your heart is telling you that you're ready to move forward."

"I don't know if I can do that, Kim. I don't know if I'll ever be ready." Becca sighed.

"Tell me about her. What's her name? Is it someone I know?"

"Yeah, I think you know of her."

"So give."

"Her name is Chase Hunter." Becca waited for it to sink in.

"No."

Becca heard Kim whistle.

"She is the hottest woman at Eastman. Damn, girl, what did you do to get her attention?"

"Honestly, I don't know. It just happened. I felt this connection to her the first time we met."

"Does she feel the same?"

"Kim, it's only the early days. She's willing to drive way out here so I guess she might be interested."

"So why are you feeling blue? You've got a hot woman interested in you. That should make you smile, not cry."

"You know why, Kim. Everyone I love I kill." Becca swallowed hard in an attempt to keep the tears at bay.

"Okay, it's time to stop the crazy talk, Becca. You love me and I'm still kicking so stop saying stupid things. You killed no one. It was an accident that had nothing to do with you."

Becca heard her friend growl.

"For once give yourself a break. Why not just let it happen with the hottie and see where it goes."

"You don't understand, Kim. I can't let it happen to anyone else."

"Oh, I understand more than you know. It's why you pushed me away so hard."

"Look, Kim, I know it was all me but that didn't mean we belonged together. We didn't fit and you know that." Becca held her hand to her head as her tears subsided. "You know I'm right don't you?"

"Yeah, I do. But it doesn't mean I still don't care about you and want to see you happy. Please, give her a chance. Don't throw something away before it even starts."

"Thanks."

"For what?"

"Talking me down." Becca closed her eyes and leaned her forehead against a pane of glass. Her eyes tracked to the deer stand and she thought she saw movement. "What was that?"

"Huh?"

"Nothing, it must be a possum or raccoon up in the deer stand. It's turning colder and they start looking for a warm place."

"You okay?"

"Yes. I'm going to get some sleep. Chase said she'd be here for breakfast and who knows how early that will be or if she even turns up."

"She'll be there. Is Chase Hunter really coming to your home for breakfast? You must have put some serious mojo on her. I have a good feeling about this, Bec."

Becca smiled. "Yeah. You know, so do I. Good night, Kim. Thanks for calling me. I needed to hear a voice of reason from someone who cares."

"Nite."

Becca disconnected the phone and whistled for Georgie. "Come on, girl, let's lock up and go to bed. I have a special friend coming tomorrow."

Just as Becca reached the bottom of the staircase, she looked at the door and shook her head. For a long moment, she stared at the keypad for the alarm.

"I didn't disarm it when I got home." Becca frowned. "All I did was set it. Did I forget to set the alarm this morning, Georgie?"

She felt a chill run through her body as she looked around the room. "Stop being paranoid, Bec, you just forgot to arm it this morning."

Becca reached for the banister and motioned for Georgie to go up the stairs. She waited a few minutes and when she didn't hear her dog bark she climbed the stairs after her.

†

The watcher blew out a sigh of relief. "A six foot raccoon indeed. Good thing she was preoccupied. I've been too careless today and that won't do. It's a good thing she didn't realize about the alarm until now." The watcher smiled. "She's going to give it a try. That is something worth reporting."

Becca was looking out her bedroom window with her hand pressing against the glass, and the watcher saw tears track her cheeks through the binoculars. After the light went out, the watcher said a fervent prayer for Becca.

"Please, Lord, let her find happiness along with the right person to make her happy." The watcher leaned back against the wall. "How I wish it could be me but I know that it's impossible."

Chapter Eleven

Becca woke with a start in the middle of the night. She had struggled to get to sleep as Kim's words mixed with Chase's smile and haunted her. She switched on the bedside light and picked up the photo album she always looked at on nights like this one. She saw a picture of her and Kim laughing.

I don't remember laughing that much since.

She turned the page and saw a picture of them with her mom and dad. She just stared at the picture noting the time stamp in the corner.

"He died the next week," she told the book flatly before flipping the page.

It was Kim who helped her through her father's death after Becca had found him on the ground in the backyard. She gave him CPR and had revived him then waited with her mother by his side until the paramedics arrived. Kim was there for her as she and her mom heard the doctor say *I'm sorry we couldn't save him. His heart was too far gone.*

Becca ran her finger across the faces. They all looked happy. She and Kim had the bloom of new lovers in their expressions. Then it all went terribly wrong. Becca knew it was because she was distant and unemotional that they broke up. It still surprised her that Kim stayed her friend and became the rock that Becca counted upon.

Now, Chase Hunter had come into her life and Becca felt the pull toward the woman instantly.

Chase is funny, kind, serious, and beautiful. What's not to like?

She punched the pillow and, turning on her side, she saw the night sky filled with twinkling stars. The view always grounded her as to just how insignificant her sorrows were in the big picture of things. But they didn't allay the memory of a year earlier when her world shattered again because of her neglect to change a stupid light bulb.

She saw a shooting star and muttered a wish. "I wish I wasn't alone anymore and can know love when I find it."

Becca closed her eyes and sleep found her.

†

Chase's eyes opened and she looked at the clock radio by her bed. *Six o'clock. I slept in late. She smiled. Wonder if it is too early to call Becca and say I'm on my way?* She got out of bed laughing and headed for the bathroom.

"I think that would mean I'm a bit desperate to see her and be alone with her outside of work."

She continued to chuckle as she turned on the shower.

If Chase was completely honest with herself, the answer would be, *yes* she was anxious to see Becca. The woman had intrigued her ever since she first laid eyes on her three years earlier. Jim Douglas never brought his PA along with him to meetings, giving her little chance to speak to Becca. And after three years of covertly watching and waiting, she was giddy with the thought of spending time privately with Becca.

Showered and dressed, Chase picked up her keys and headed for the parking garage. It was only six-forty-five and just getting light when her silver BMW entered the almost deserted street. "I'll get myself some coffee from the coffee place on the way and drive slow."

She looked at the GPS screen and noticed that the estimated time of arrival at Becca's place was forty-five minutes.

"I'll get there around eight…that's a good time to surprise her."

✝

Chase's car rolled to a stop in front of Becca's home and she exited her car. Her eyes tracked around the area and she saw a stand of birch along with some sort of pine tree. She wasn't much for flora and fauna and only recognized the birch trees because she recalled reading a book about Indians using the bark for canoes. The yard was tidy with a row of flowers on either side of the porch steps. To Chase's right was a shed and a deer stand nestled in another stand of trees.

For fifteen minutes, Chase stood and watched the house looking for any sign of movement. She knew Becca had a dog and she hadn't heard any barking.

Maybe getting here so early was a mistake. She turned to open the car door and stopped. *I'm not leaving. This is where I want to be.*

Chase leaned against her car, pulled her cell phone out of her pocket, and dialed Becca's number.

✝

Becca didn't want to open her eyes at the insistent ringing of her phone. Her eyes flew open. "Oh, shit! Chase." Her eyes widened as she saw it was eight o'clock. "Hello."

"Did I wake you up?"

"Um," Becca yawned. "Yeah, you caught me but I will have the coffee ready by the time you get here."

"I'm here."

Becca heard Chase laugh.

"You're here now? No way."

Becca untangled herself from the sheets and walked to the front window. What she saw made her smile. There was Chase Hunter leaning against her car with her arms crossed and her legs crossed at the ankles. Chase waved.

"I'll be right down to open the door.

By the time Becca got to the front door, Georgie was already sitting by it with her stubby tail thumping. "You could have warned me when she got here you know."

Becca turned off the alarm and opened the door. The sight of Chase standing there made her catch her breath. "Good morning. Breakfast isn't ready yet but the coffee should be."

"You looked mighty cute in the window but up close…" Chase shook her head. "You look even cuter."

Becca laughed and opened the door wide.

Chase immediately crouched down to give the jumping dog a scratch.

"That's Georgette.

"Hey there, girl." Chase scratched the dog behind her ears and Georgie immediately flopped to the floor and turned so she could get a belly rub."

Chase laughed. "She's a great dog. She doesn't shed, does she?"

"No, that's the beauty of a poodle mix." Becca was very aware of her erect nipples pushing against her T-shirt in the coolness of the morning air. "Umm. Let me show you to the mugs and coffee then I will take a quick shower and get dressed."

Chase stood.

"Okay, but you don't have to get dressed on my account." She winked and moved past Becca. "From the moment I saw your house I knew why you want to live here."

Chase looked around the living room. "It's very cozy and charming."

"Thanks. Come with me and I'll get you that coffee." Becca pulled a lightweight jacket off the coat rack and put it on. "It's a bit chilly this morning."

She looked at Chase dressed in jeans, a dark green sweater with a white shirt collar was peeking out. "I see you are, as always, dressed perfectly for the occasion."

She touched the coffee pot, pulled the cupboard door above it open, fetched a mug and poured some coffee into it. "There's sugar in the bowl and creamer is in the fridge. I hope you like hazelnut or vanilla." She turned and saw that Chase had a grin on her face. "What?"

"Either is good. I'd say I was sorry I didn't warn you that I was on my way earlier but I'm not." Her grin grew wider as she took the cup from Becca. "I think it was the fresh eggs that were being laid that occupied my mind."

Becca laughed. "Well, those will have to wait until I get dressed."

"Do you have a basket to put them in?"

"Of course."

"Then while you're getting ready, I will make myself useful and gather the eggs."

"You are going to gather the eggs?" Becca looked at Chase skeptically.

"Yep. You are looking at a farm girl born and raised."

"Really? Wow. Well, okay then, I'll get you the basket and point out the chicken coop."

Becca walked into the mudroom, picked up the basket, and handed it to Chase. Through the window in the door, she pointed to what was obviously the chicken coop.

"You're sure you want to do this?"

Chase nodded.

"Then have at it."

She opened the door and Georgie took off only to stop and sit on the grass.

"Georgie will show you the way."

Chase's hand brushed the skin on Becca's arm as she took the basket. "I'll be back with a basketful by the time you are done getting ready."

†

Becca stood at the door window watching Chase and Georgie romp toward the chicken coop. The revelation that Chase grew up on a farm surprised her but if she considered what her upbringing was, she shouldn't be. It was clear by the way Chase entered the chicken coop she knew what she was doing.

"I hope that granny chicken doesn't peck her too hard. Guess I better get myself ready for the day." Becca took another long look at her new friend and her dog and grinned.

In the shower, Becca couldn't get the image of Chase leaning against her car out of her mind. She looked too sexy and Becca couldn't deny her attraction to the woman. Nor could she stop the flutters in her stomach as she remembered the low sexy timber to Chase's voice. A shiver ran through her whole body and made her tremble when Chase's hand brushed her arm. Becca thought she'd die on the spot because of the intensity in her body that the touch created

"I think I can get used to having her around and never be sad again. She does make me smile." Becca turned off the shower, dried off and put her clothes on hurriedly—she couldn't wait to get back downstairs and see Chase again.

†

The one thing about being on a farm that Chase detested was cleaning the chicken coop. Just the recalled smell made her stomach lurch. But, she told Becca she'd gather the eggs and she prepared for the stench as she opened the door to the coop. It surprised her that what she recalled was not the smell associated with this chicken coop. All she smelled was fresh straw and as she peered inside, she saw neatly arranged nesting boxes.

"Wow, this is something else."

Chase's eyes scanned the area and again she marveled at how clean it was. *Did she get up in the middle of the night and clean this place? Is that why she slept so late?*

Chase went about the business of gathering the eggs from the nesting boxes. Most of the chickens were already outside after exiting the minute she opened the door. Two holdouts refused to budge when she reached under them for eggs. One had no eggs and the other made quick and constant pecks at her hand. In one swift move, Chase picked the hen up and let it go on the floor before she picked up two fresh, warm brown eggs.

When she turned to leave the enclosure and her eyes met Becca's staring at her from outside the chicken wire. "Duty finished and I have a nice amount of eggs for you." Chase smiled. "I must say your coop is far superior to any I encountered on the farm growing up."

"I can't take credit for that. I remembered the awful smell from my childhood and hire someone to do it for me."

Becca laughed as Chase joined her. She immediately saw the back of Chase's hand that had a few bloody spots and grinned. "I see I should have warned you about my granny chicken."

Chase looked at her hand. "It is nothing. She was holding out with two of the bigger eggs."

"Well then, they will be yours for breakfast."

The two women climbed the stairs to the porch and the door.

"What is your pleasure? You want a real country breakfast or something lighter?" Becca asked.

Chase chuckled. "The last time I was back at home on the farm it was Christmas, so that is the last country breakfast I've had."

"Then it is time for another, don't you think?"

"Sounds good to me." Chase's face grew serious. "I was almost up close and personal with a buck today."

"You're not hurt are you?"

"No." Chase grinned. "Thanks for the concern. You know the place where you go down a hill and go along with pasture on both sides?"

Becca nodded."

"I looked to my right and I saw him running across the field at full speed. I slowed down and was about two car lengths away when he darted across the road."

"Wow! Good thing you saw him. Imagine what would have happened if it were dark."

"I know. Hey, whatever you are making sure smells wonderful.

✝

While eating the enormous breakfast, Chase sighed often. "This so reminds me of home."

"Where is home? Around here?" Becca asked as she spread jam on her biscuit.

"No. Home is in Wisconsin. My folks are dairy farmers." Chase patted her stomach. "That was great."

"Thanks. Do you have brothers or sisters, Chase?"

"Yep. Four of each. How about you?"

"Nope, I am the last of my family line."

Chase heard the sadness in Becca's voice. "How did that happen?"

Becca knitted her eyebrows. "They all died…"

"No, not what I meant."

"Then what?"

Chase swallowed at what was obviously a sore point and something Becca didn't want to share. "I'm sorry. I wasn't prying. I just was wondering if there is a distant cousin or anything like that. With all the ancestry stuff out there I figured it wouldn't be hard to find something like that out."

Chase saw Becca narrow her eyes. "Oops, guess I said way too much."

"No. No, not at all. I hadn't thought of that. The curse of my family is they only have one child. Both my parents were only children as were both of their parents. I never thought to find something like that out. I suppose it wouldn't take too much time." Becca's shoulders relaxed. "Are all your siblings high powered executives like you? Or did some stay on the farm."

"I'm the only one who wanted to be off the farm. With each birth, my dad would buy a section of land and put the new baby's name on it. Then when they turned eighteen, he would let them borrow his equipment to start a farm of their own. All my brothers took him up on the offer and after my sisters married they built houses on their section and their husbands started farming."

"Dairy farmers too?" Becca asked.

"Mostly but a few of them grow corn as well."

"So somewhere in Wisconsin there is a section of land named *Chase*?" Becca grinned.

Chase sighed. "No, I gave it back." She brought her coffee mug to her lips and swallowed some of the dark brew. "To be honest, after seeing your place here it kinda makes me regret not holding on to the land."

Becca sat silently then shook her head. "Not if farming wasn't what you wanted."

"It never was. While all my brothers and sisters were doing the 4H thing, I was out playing basketball."

"Ah yes, *4H—head, heart, hands, and health.* I was a member of that for all of a month…just couldn't get into all that farm stuff everyone around me was so crazy about." Becca looked past Chase's shoulder. "Not much of a joiner I guess." Her gaze returned to Chase. "Why basketball?"

"I knew my family couldn't afford to send me to a university and there was no way I could make enough money on my own so I became the best girls' basketball player in Wisconsin." Chase shrugged. "It got me through my undergraduate degree."

"And after that did you go to work for Eastman?"

"Initially, as an intern during my last semester. I guess they saw something there because after two years they sent me to Harvard School of Business for my MBA."

"Wow that is impressive. You must have been very young when you became a vice president."

Chase felt her cheeks heat up. "Enough about me. I've read your personnel file and see that you are on the fast track within the company as well."

Becca's eyes widened. "Really? I didn't know that."

"Actually, Douglas did you a favor in making you do most of his work. It hasn't gone unnoticed, Becca." Chase put her hands on the table and stood. "Why don't we do the dishes and then I seem to remember the promise of a tour of your property…and maybe the house too."

Becca grinned and picked up her plate before she too stood. "Did you bring a jacket? It will get breezy in the buggy I have."

Chapter Twelve

"You ready to go?" Becca asked as she put on her jacket and gloves.

"Right behind you. By the way, thanks for lending me a jacket. Obviously I didn't think ahead when you talked about a tour of your property." Chase laughed. "Guess I was thinking of some sort of heated tour bus."

"Ah, you just wait, Ms. Hunter, until you see my little beast of a touring bus. Your feet will be warm at least." Becca opened the door and followed Chase out.

Chase pointed to the deer stand. "Do you go hunting?"

Becca shook her head. "No. No, my dad was the hunter. I'd tag along whenever I got the chance but I just never could bring myself to kill anything." She felt a slight hitch in her voice. "He only shot what we would eat but I can still feel the bile in my throat whenever I remember seeing a live deer fall to the ground dead."

"My dad is a big hunter too. He'd take us all, one by one, with him and taught us how to shoot a rifle and where the right place was to aim for. He always said there was nothing to gain by just injuring an animal and if you were going to kill something, to do it with the best shot possible."

Chase put her arm around Becca's shoulder. "I never could bring myself to kill anything either. I was happy with tin cans."

Becca pointed to the deer stand. "No one has used that thing since my dad passed away. Up there you can see a clearing where deer come to eat. Dad said it was because the grasses were so sweet they couldn't resist and that gave him an added bonus of not having to haul what he shot too far." Becca smiled at the memory. "There's the barn where my beast is."

"Come on, I'll race you." Chase sprinted toward the building.

"Hey, no fair." Becca grabbed Chase around the waist, pushed her aside, and ran past her. "I'm first. Ha."

Chase put her hands on her knees and sucked in a breath of cool air. "You work out or jog or something? I thought I was in pretty good shape."

Becca saw the adorable pout on Chase's face and had to resist pulling her in for a hug. Instead, she pushed open the barn door. "There she is—my yellow hornet."

Chase laughed. "It's a freakin' yellow dune buggy."

"Shh, don't let her hear you say the *DB* word. If she does, we are guaranteed to find every ditch and dip around the entire two-hundred and fifty acres."

"Does she have seatbelts?"

Becca slapped Chase's arm. "Of course she does. I've tricked her out with all the best money can buy."

"Is there a speaker system so you can narrate as you drive…unless you'd rather I drive?"

Becca studied Chase. "I would but you don't know the way and I do."

"Ah, but I can follow directions."

"Can I be honest with you?"

"Of course. Is something wrong?"

Becca looked at the ground. "You should know that I have only invited one other person out here. I don't have a lot of close friends."

Chase frowned. "I can't believe that. You are one of the most liked and popular personal assistants at Eastman."

"I'm not talking about work. That's just superficial. My friend Kim is the only person who I've let into this, my private life."

"Does she work at Eastman?"

"Yes. Her last name is Richardson."

"She has red hair," Chase raised her hand. "And is about this tall, right? And she's part of the secretarial pool at Eastman, right?"

Becca's eyes widened. "You know her?"

"I know of her. Have you been friends long?"

"Yes, she is a dear friend who has been there for me no matter what." Becca lifted her eyes, gazed in Chase's before swallowing hard. "It's weird. I've known you for only a matter of days and I feel as though I've known you forever."

Chase took a step closer. "What's even weirder is that I feel the same draw to you."

She scratched her nose before a brief smile appeared on her face. "You should know that I have watched you from a distance for several years now."

Becca frowned. "Really? I can't recall ever seeing you before this past Wednesday a week ago. Were you stalking me?"

A rich laugh came from deep in Chase's throat. "No, I wasn't stalking you. Douglas never brought you to any of the staff meetings or special occasions. I was curious as to why and asked him. He told me *her place is in her office working*. I knew the kind of numbers his team had and suspected he didn't generate it all."

Becca couldn't stop the skeptical look she was sure was on her face.

"So I looked at your personnel file and was impressed. Then I wondered what you looked like. The colored four by six was missing and the only picture in your file was grainy and almost impossible to see."

"Sort of like your driver's license picture?"

"Exactly. I made some excuse to visit Jim in his office so I could see you for myself. I was looking for the reason why he always kept you out of the loop. If you were too heavy, not pretty, or had some disability, I wanted to know so I could bring it to the attention of the folks in human resources."

"Why?" Becca asked suspiciously.

"That is a good question and to be honest, I don't know the answer as to the why. I think I didn't trust him. And I had this desperate need to see you. I just did." Chase shrugged.

"When I visited Jim, you were sitting at your desk with you head bent then raised it when you had a phone call." Chase's cheeks blushed. "You were the most beautiful woman I'd ever seen." She smiled. "I was bewitched from that moment on."

"I'm confused. Why didn't you just come into my office and introduce yourself instead of watching me for years?" Becca asked.

"Douglas always insisted on walking me to the elevator. Even when I said it wasn't necessary he still followed behind me." Chase cocked her head to the left. "After that he was on my radar."

"If he didn't want me out and about, why did he let me do the prelim with you for Knox?"

A full smile filled Chase's face. "Because I called and insisted that you do it. I didn't give him a choice. I recalled thinking he sounded relived that I asked for you and not him."

"Of course he was. I hadn't fully prepped him at that point." Becca finally felt her shoulders relax. "I have one more confession."

Chase raised her left eyebrow. "And it is?"

"I haven't driven the beast in more than a year and I think I will take you up on your offer to drive while I narrate."

"Okay. Why haven't you?"

Becca looked away. "Too many memories," she whispered.

Chase wrapped an arm around Becca's shoulders. "We don't have to tour." Her voice was soft and full of tenderness.

"No. I want to show you." Becca shrugged. "It's time I put things to rest."

✝

Chase drove as the beast bumped up and down the dirt road. She liked the sound of Becca's voice as she pointed out various areas and added a personal story of why she liked the place. Chase wanted to ask what things Becca needed to put to rest but resisted. The sadness and pain in her eyes was evident and she didn't see any reason to stir up whatever caused it. *Maybe in time she will open up to me.*

"Stop up there around the next bend in the road." Becca pointed to an area ahead on the right.

Chase stopped and turned toward Becca.

"Other than the area around my house, this is my favorite place on the property. Come on, I'll show you." Becca waited for Chase to meet her then took her hand and guided her down a hill that was hiding a small pond. "My folks and I would come here in the evening during the summer when it was the hottest. Mom would pack a picnic basket and we'd sit on a quilt and just enjoyed the breeze coming across the water."

"Are there fish in there?" Chase pointed her chin toward the water.

"Shoot, I should have remembered to bring some poles. They were always in the beast until my dad passed. Next time you come out we will go fishing."

"So, there will be a next time?" Chase felt her heart pounding in her chest as she held her breath.

Becca narrowed her eyes before she grinned. "Of course." Her brow furrowed. "Did you doubt it?"

Chase let out her breath. "Well, I had hoped."

For a long moment, Becca stared at Chase. "Somehow I doubt that someone as successful as you are, Ms. Hunter, *hope*s more than *knows*."

"Guilty as charged except where you are concerned. It is a very disconcerting feeling and one that I am not entirely comfortable with."

Becca grabbed Chase's hand again. "Come on, let me show you something."

Chase laughed and went along with whatever it was that Becca wanted to do. She was in such a good mood and she knew nothing would change that as long as she was with Becca. The woman made her feel free and happy.

"Where are you taking me?"

"You'll see." Becca laughed. "It wouldn't be a surprise if I told you now, would it?"

They moved quickly along a narrow path around the water. Becca stopped at a clearing and turned to Chase. "This is where we'd always stay."

She pointed to the natural clearing with a large flat rock. "If you look in that direction late in the day you can see the most spectacular sunsets. My mom said the sky was painted by the fairies just for us."

Chase saw a wistful look cross Becca's face as she seemed lost in her memories. Still she saw an underlying sadness that she wished she could help Becca overcome. With all the tenderness she had, Chase slipped her hand back into Becca's hand.

"I imagine it was a magical time for you and your folks."

Becca smiled. "Yes it was. Do you have memories like that about your family?"

"To tell you the truth, there was nothing as special as your memories. There were too many of us. I mean I have happy memories of family time but nothing like this. My folks did what they could but with nine kids there was not a lot of one-on-one time."

"Now that you are away from them and time has passed, do you regret not staying behind with your family?"

Chase laughed. "No. I knew I'd never get married—to a man anyway. I think my folks love me no matter who I loved but when I said I wasn't going to be a farmer I'm pretty sure they were relieved. I don't think they wanted to explain my queerness to their friends anymore."

"Hmm, did that make you feel bad? I mean were they embarrassed about your life style?"

Chase shrugged. "I wasn't out or anything like that but I knew there was speculation. Just before I left for college, I told them and by their expressions, I knew they weren't surprised. What about your folks, how did they feel or did they even know?"

"They knew and loved me anyway. My dad used to say, *it's who you are that matters not who you love*. I think they were disappointed that there wouldn't be any grandchildren from me."

Silence ensured for a minute until Becca touched Chase's hand. "I don't know about you, but I'm getting hungry." Becca's stomach rumbled.

"Me too. Shall we head back?"

"Yes, a hot cup of coffee would taste so good about now." Becca held out her hand. "I'll drive. I know a shortcut."

"Then let's get going. I can't feel my toes anymore."

Becca winked. "Well, once we get the beast going your feet will warm up right away."

"Come on, I'll race you."

†

Chase surreptitiously watched Becca as she drove across rough ground toward her home. There was no doubt about it—Becca was beautiful. Unlike many gorgeous women, Becca seemed unaware of her effect on others. The revelation that Becca had few friends surprised and puzzled Chase.

What is it that makes you so sad, Becca? You have it all. You're smart, kind, selfless, and on top of all that, you are stunningly gorgeous.

"This is one of my favorite sites on the property," Becca said pointing to a clearing of lush grasses.

"Is this the place you'd see from the deer stand?"

"Yes. In the springtime it is filled with all types of wildflowers and if you watch long enough you will see a doe bring her newborn fawn to have their first taste of the sweet grasses." Becca's face softened. "I can remember one time, I watched, fascinated by, the birth of a fawn. It was amazing to see life come in to the world," she said wistfully.

"What changed?" Chase asked.

Becca frowned. "What do you mean?"

Chase had to think fast to defuse a situation that Becca obviously didn't want to speak about. "I used the wrong word. What I meant was…do you go up in the deer stand in the spring or did something stop you from going up there."

"Oh." Becca stopped the beast. "I didn't have anyone to share it with." She looked at Chase and her eyes seemed to be pleading for understanding.

112

A big grin crossed Chase's face. "If you want, come spring I'd like to see that with you."

"Really? You'd do that for me?"

"Yes, really. I'd do that and more for you. All you need to do is ask." Chase reached out and took Becca's hand. "So what's for dinner?"

"Worked up an appetite running, did you?" Becca laughed.

"You do know I let you win." Chase winked then nodded.

"Yeah, right." She pushed on the pedal and moved the beast forward. "I have some beautiful looking New York strip steaks, baked potatoes and I think a nice green salad will round out the meal."

Chase's stomach growled and she blushed. "Sounds delicious."

✝

The watcher kept an eye on Becca all day and was now standing inside the deer stand as Becca parked her vehicle in the barn. It had been a long time since the watcher heard Becca divulge anything about her upbringing. Even the redhead probably didn't know some of the things Becca revealed to the woman who was spending the day with her.

A broad smile crossed the watcher's face. "Finally, Becca's time has come. She is with who she should be with."

✝

Chase pushed her plate away. "That was by far the best steak I've ever had. What market do you buy from?"

Becca grinned. "Actually, except for the twenty-five acres around the house, I lease the land to a local cattle

113

rancher. Part of the payment is half a cow. So whenever my freezer gets low, I'll call him. He picks out one of the better heifers in his herd and he sends it to a meat packing company. His cows are grass fed and finished so what I get is meat free of antibiotics, growth hormones and things like that."

"That is why it's so good?"

Becca nodded. "That and the fact that the aging process isn't rushed."

"Because the longer it ages the more tender the meat."

"Exactly."

"Mind if I come and have dinner with you every night?

Becca stood and started to clear the table. "You are always welcome here."

"Is tomorrow too soon?" Chase grinned.

"In that case you should spend the night."

Becca enjoyed Chase's company, feeling emotions of happiness and contentment that she hadn't felt since—forever. Even as a child, Becca was restless. She kept looking for something but didn't know exactly what. Until that moment, Becca didn't know but looking at Chase, she felt her heart soar. For the first time she was at peace.

Chase sat quietly staring at Becca before she scraped back her chair and picked up her plate. "You cooked, I clean up. Go sit and enjoy your wine."

"I can't do that. It wouldn't be right to invite you to dinner and have you do the dishes."

Becca's insides were trembling since Chase didn't reply to her comment.

"Please, it will only take me a few minutes." She looked at the bewildered look on Chase's face. "I'm sorry, if I've offended you. Like I said, I don't entertain much."

"You haven't offended me, Becca. I wanted to thank you for a delicious meal by doing the dishes." Chase shrugged. "If that is not how it's done in your home then I will sit still and watch you as you work."

"Tell you what, why don't you go make yourself comfortable in the front room and I will finish up here then we can have some coffee."

Chase shrugged. "Sure, I can do that."

†

As Chase sat waiting for Becca and the coffee, she rehashed the past few minutes in the kitchen and tried to make sense of why Becca had suddenly changed. She slapped her forehead. *Crap. She asked me to spend the night and I sat there like a lump. I think we'd better have the talk.*

"Here you go. A steaming cup of coffee along with a few homemade cookies that I hope you'll like."

Chase heard the cool tone and her body slumped in the chair. "Listen, Becca, I'd like to explain something to you."

"Sure, go ahead." Becca refused to look up.

"I think we both feel this strong attraction to one another. Would you agree?"

Becca nodded but she still refused to raise her head.

"Technically, as the Vice President of Acquisitions at Eastman, I shouldn't be here at all since I am essentially your boss." Chase saw Becca swipe at her eyes. "But…"

"There is always a *but* isn't there?" Becca whispered.

"Please look at me, Becca. Please."

Becca lifted her head and looked directly at Chase.

"Thank you."

Chase fixed her eyes on Becca's and refused to release them. "But, I can't and won't stay away. You are where I've wanted to be ever since I saw you that one day. The reason I didn't approach you and ask you out was because it is frowned upon for executives to fraternize with those who worked for them. Then, you came into my office and I knew the moment you walked in the door that I would follow you anywhere. It is you, Becca that I've been looking for all my life."

When she saw the tears in Becca's eyes, Chase got up before kneeling in front of her. "Becca, have I said something wrong?

"No," Becca sobbed. "You've said everything right. It's like you've looked into my heart and heard my prayers."

Chase stood and pulled Becca to her. "And you have heard mine. I can't spend the night right now. Not until I sort some things out first."

"There's someone else?"

Chase placed a soft kiss on Becca's forehead. "There is no one else and hasn't been for a very long time."

"Then why?

Chase took Becca's hand and led her to the sofa. "Please, sit with me." When Becca was sitting by her side, Chase took her hand again. "Right now, in my department, Acquisitions, there is an opening for one team leader…he was the one who sent you the rose and note."

"You fired him?"

Chase nodded.

"Ross comes in tomorrow to empty his office." Chase squeezed Becca's hand. "We'd been looking to get rid of him for some time now because of all the sexual harassment charges. All of those were *he said she said* until he sent you that note. The unfortunate part is that he was an excellent manager but the irrefutable evidence of his activities made it impossible for Eastman to keep him on since he was becoming a liability. It was time for him to go."

"Isn't there some rule about you telling me this?" Becca asked.

"Probably. Because of what is happening between us I need you to understand what is happening at Eastman. The last thing I want to do is give you mixed messages."

"About what?"

Chase swallowed hard. She was on shaky ground and knew it. "About…" She looked into Becca's beautiful eyes. "Fraternization between bosses and their subordinates is frowned upon. Not forbidden, since I know for a fact it has happened, but the impact on your position is what I worry the most about."

Becca moved very close to Chase. "I'm a big girl and can take of myself. You need not worry about me."

"Until we met, in what seems like years ago to me, your name was the top of the list for replacing Jim Douglas."

"I didn't know he was leaving. Did he get another job?"

"No, I am considering him for another position."

"You mean like a promotion?" Becca looked confused.

"No. He isn't getting a promotion." Chase shook her head. "It is more of a sideways move."

"So what's the problem? I still don't understand."

Chase sighed. "Now, after today I don't know what to do."

"What do you mean by *after today*?" Becca squeezed Chase's hand. "You felt it too."

"Yes. And as much as I'd like to stay and be here for you all the time, I need to make sure things for you at Eastman are solid."

Becca leaned in and gave Chase a feather light kiss. "I will not take any position if it compromises your integrity with the company." She kissed Chase again. "Let's see where this—" She waved a hand between them. "Goes and take it slow." Becca held out a hand. "Deal?"

Chase ginned. "A kiss will seal the deal." She then took Becca in her arms and kissed her with all the passion she was feeling.

†

The watcher brushed away tears as Becca and Chase held one another as they stood by Chase's car.

"My little one, be happy. This woman is *the one* you've been praying for."

That night when Becca went to bed, she stood at the window but didn't raise her hand. Instead, a glorious smile curved her lips.

Chapter Thirteen

Becca drove to work, her mind on one thing and one thing only—Chase Hunter. She wondered how they would act toward one another in the work environment. True, their paths didn't cross often except for that one time that fate brought them together in her office. *It seems like I've known her forever.*

Her phone rang and she answered it expecting one of the team to call or Mr. Douglas to chew her out for something or another. Becca was certain he wouldn't call her if what Chase said were true. Instead, Becca heard static and as she strained to hear, she was sure she could hear a voice saying her name.

"You'll have to speak up. I can't hear what you're saying." The static continued to the point where she could hear nothing else. "Call me back," she yelled before she disconnected the Bluetooth connection.

Becca smiled. Chase had called her Saturday night to say she got home without a deer encounter and to thank her again for the glorious day. And it had been a glorious day. Sunday, Becca paced around the house trying to decide if it was too forward to call Chase just to say hi and see how her day was going. She finally decided that she'd wait and see if Chase called her—she didn't. By the time Becca decided she would call Chase, it was too late to call so she gave up and went to bed disappointed in herself for her lack of courage.

†

Just as Becca parked her car and was ready to exit it, her phone rang again. "If this is that same static crap I'm getting a new number." She pressed the Bluetooth answer button. "Hello."

"Good morning, Becca."

A grin crossed Becca's lips. "Well, good morning to you too, Chase."

"How long before you get to work?"

The rumble in Chase's voice made Becca shiver. "Just getting out of my car now. What do you have in mind?"

"Why don't you bypass your floor and come to my office. Debra won't be in yet so just come straight to my office if you'd like."

"I'd like. I've thought about you all weekend and wanted to call you but I chickened out."

"Why?"

"I didn't want to appear too anxious." Becca laughed. "I guess by telling you that now my secret is out."

A rich laugh came from Chase just as Becca boarded the elevator car.

"To tell you the truth, I was in the same quandary. Call or not call. I guess we both lost out because I really wanted to hear your voice."

"I'm in the elevator now."

"I'm standing in front of it waiting. Are there many people in there with you?"

"No, it's just me with two floors to go."

When the bell chimed that she'd reached Chase's floor and the door slid open, Becca felt her heart flutter and pleasure fill her body. The sight of Chase made her finally understand the meaning of swoon.

†

Chase grabbed Becca's hand and walked quickly to her office. Once inside she closed the door and locked it. "You do know that I am known as the *ice bitch* around here, don't you?"

Becca nodded.

"You, my dear Becca, have completely destroyed that image."

"For everyone?"

"No, only for you." Chase pulled Becca near and kissed the soft lips that captured her attention.

Becca leaned into the kiss.

Chase opened her mouth, traced Becca's lips with her tongue, and melted into her as their tongues danced. When they pulled apart, they sighed in unison. "I've been thinking of nothing else since I left your place Saturday night."

"We were in sync then. You should have spent the night."

"As appealing as the thought of making love with you is, Becca, I don't think we should rush things." She grinned. "We haven't even gotten to know one another. Like what your favorite movie is or what you like on pizza."

Becca caressed Chase's cheek. "For me, it seems like I've always known you." She kissed waiting lips then pulled back. "Will you have dinner with me on Wednesday night, as in a date?"

"Are you cooking again?" Chase wiggled her eyebrows. "I mean cooking food of course."

"Of course." Becca grinned. "No, as in I want to take you out to dinner at a restaurant."

"Why Wednesday and not today?"

"Wednesday is when my housekeeper comes and I know she will let Georgie out so I won't need to run right home after work."

"Then, I'd love to go out on a date with you on Wednesday. Do you have any place special in mind? Maybe my place."

Becca laughed. "I think not. Right now I'd like to undress you so imagine what would happen if we were alone in your apartment."

"I'd be good."

"But I won't and we just agreed to take it slow."

They kissed again and this time it was deep and sensual.

Chase's phone rang.

"Don't get it," Becca said as her hand grazed Chase's left breast.

Chase took a step back. "It is probably Debra wanting to see if I am here. If I don't answer she will come and unlock the door, open the blinds and start my coffee maker."

"You sure have a cushy life." Becca followed Chase to her desk and continued kissing her neck.

"Hello," Chase managed to say. "Yes, I'm here... Will you please call Ed Eastman's office and schedule an appointment for me with him as soon as possible?... Thanks, Debra."

With a trembling hand, Chase hung up the phone and pulled Becca to her. "Is this how you treat all your lovers?"

"Nope." Becca began nibbling Chase's ear. "In fact, if you asked any of my past girlfriends—there aren't that many—they'd all say I was rather cold and unresponsive. I heard that from each of them when we parted ways." Becca stepped back.

"And, I'm different how?"

Becca laughed. "Because you are so damn sexy and you make me feel things I had no idea I could feel."

"Then that makes two of us." Chase let go of Becca and sighed. "As much as I'd like to keep you here with me all day, I do have work to do."

"I know, so do I. We probably broke all kinds of rules by being here alone."

"None that I'll report." Chase went to her desk and pulled out a packet of papers in a sealed envelope. "I've put Douglas on administrative leave for two weeks so you need not worry about him again. I'd like you to take control of the team. This is the next acquisition we are thinking of and I'd like you and your team to see what you can come up with."

Becca accepted the envelope. "I'll meet with them first thing. We usually have an informal meeting with coffee after everyone gets here. Do you want me to tell them about Mr. Douglas?" Becca held the envelope tight.

"No, I sent them all a personal email to let them know what the situation with Douglas is and that in the interim you would be acting manager."

"Who gets to kiss the *ice bitch*?"

"Exactly. I'll walk you to the elevator. I have a big day ahead and it doesn't look good for me to fire a manager so I need to get personnel in place as soon as I can."

Chase put her arm around Becca's shoulders and kissed her cheek as they walked to the door. "The search for a new manager will generate a lot of talk and probably some of it will be about you and me. Rick Ross was very vocal so be prepared. I will try to head it off before it goes full steam ahead."

"Look, if being with me is a problem, I will back off. I won't like it but I certainly don't want to be an embarrassment for you." Becca looked away.

"No. Don't even think that, Becca. I've waited too long for you to come into my life and I'm not letting you go."

Becca shrugged. "Perhaps you'll find I'm not what you thought I am. I do have a pretty poor record when it comes to girlfriends."

Chase turned Becca and lifted her chin. "I don't care about the past, only the future. I know you feel it too. We can't deny what we feel for one another. I know it's only been a short time but when I hold you, I feel like I could spontaneously explode and that goes for whenever you are near." She held Becca's chin refusing to let her look away. "Tell me you don't feel the same."

A lone tear rolled down Becca's cheek. "I can't tell you that for it would be a lie. Still I don't want to be in the way."

"You will *never* be in my way." Chase searched Becca's eyes. "Trust me."

"I do."

†

Chase rapped on Edward Eastman's door when she heard him bid her *enter*, she twisted the knob before pushing it open.

"Chase, come sit and tell me what you need."

Edward wasn't a particularly big man but his presence made him seem larger than life. He had gray eyes, a full head of steel gray hair along with a heavy moustache, all giving the impression of power.

He walked around his desk and pointed to a chair in front of his desk. "Please, Chase, take a seat."

Chase took the seat and Edward turned the chair next to hers and sat down.

"Now, tell me what I can do for you."

"Thanks for letting me meet with you so quickly. The fact that I've had to fire Ross looks bad for me but more importantly for the company."

Edward nodded. "Ross was an embarrassment and a liability to the company's reputation. You had no other option but to terminate him."

"What I suggest we do is have a few headhunters look discreetly into who they might have to fill the position. Also, I think it would be wise to open the job to all of the Eastman PA's."

"Good idea. I've had my eye on two of them for some time now that I think would make top rate managers."

Chase felt her stomach turn. "Care to share?"

Edward smiled what some might call a fatherly smile. "Number one is Becca Cameron. It's clear she has been carrying Douglas's load for some time now."

A volcano went off in Chase's stomach. "And the other?"

"Dustin Stewart. He is very capable and has had a hand in pulling some questionable acquisitions out of the fire and on to our side when Ross could not."

Chase nodded. "I agree that the two are exemplary in their jobs. I am going to put Jim Douglas into Ross' position. Perhaps he will come to understand that if he is to succeed he needs to do the work. Ross' team doesn't have a strong PA since Ross did most of the work himself."

"We shall see on that front. If he doesn't step up to the challenge then he will be out looking for a new job. At his age and salary requirements a new job won't be easy for him to find." He smiled fondly at Chase. "Once you've notified him of his new position, have him make an appointment with me and I will make sure he knows the lay of the land so to speak."

"Thank you. I'd appreciate that since he is a true chauvinist." Chase took a minute to gather her thoughts.

"Unfortunately, we need to go through the charade of looking outside the company when we have two qualified applicants within Eastman."

Edward's gray eyes fixed on Chase and she felt very uncomfortable.

"That is how the game is played, is it not?" Chase asked.

"Yes, it is." Edward cleared his throat. "We've known one another a long time, Chase. I can remember you as a young intern and thinking *she is going places*. Frankly, I do not care how one conducts their lives as long as it does not impinge on the company. Do you remember the talk we had about ten years ago?"

"You mean the one where I came out to you just before I became a manager?"

Edward nodded. "And do you remember what I said?"

"It made no difference to you as long as I did my job." Chase's cheeks flushed. "Therein lays the problem. I am romantically involved with Becca Cameron. She is the most qualified and capable PA we have to handle Douglas's job but if I give her the job, the rumor mill will run rampant. I won't do that to Eastman."

"I already have had an earful about you and Ms. Cameron from Ross during his exit interview." Edward tapped his fingers together. "But, denying Ms. Cameron the job will not be what is best for Eastman. I've had my eye on Ms. Cameron since she came to work here. Just as I saw great things in your future, I see the same in hers."

"Then, what shall I do?" Chase waited as Edward continued to tap his fingers.

"You will do nothing. I will assign Bob Kellerman and Vonda Polanski along with two people from HR to conduct a search within and outside of Eastman to find the most qualified candidates for interviews. Once they make a final decision, I will interview each selectee personally and the decision will be ultimately mine. That way you will have no hand in my decision."

"That sounds fair." Chase shrugged. "It will look bad if I'm not on the committee but your plan will certainly keep the busy bodies quiet." Chase looked away. "You should know that I appointed Douglas's PA as the interim manager. It makes sense since there will be continuity until a permanent manager is hired."

"Excellent. Just keep an eye on her to make sure she is doing what you expect of her."

"She did everything for Douglas so she knows how to run an acquisition proposal."

Edward smiled his fatherly smile again. "In all the years I've known you, you've never let your personal life interfere with your work and I don't see that happening now."

"Thank you, sir. I'd quit before I'd let that happen."

Edward's eyes seemed to be studying her and Chase slowed her breathing refusing to squirm.

"She means that much to you?"

"Yes."

Edward stood and held his hand out to Chase. When she stood, he dropped his hand and engulfed her in his arms. "I'm happy for you."

✝

Chase left the executive suite smiling. Edward Eastman let her see a side of him that not many did. He was a man of few words who wielded an iron fist over his company. But for Chase, he gave his blessing and an out.

If they pick Becca, which I expect they will, there will be no gossip about her getting the job because she's sleeping with me. She's not yet but she will be or I'm way off base.

Even though there was a pile of work for her on her desk, Chase decided to visit each of the PA's turned temporary managers and see if they needed anything or were having any problems. She normally would let someone else handle the situation but it was a way to see Becca again without garnering suspicion.

✝

Chase stood in the hallway just outside of what was Rick Ross' office and watched as Dustin Steward, the PA she had temporarily assigned as the acting manager, read a paper seemingly perplexed by the document. She rapped lightly on the doorframe and Dustin raised his head with a startled look.

"Dustin, how are you?" Chase hid her amusement at the look on his face.

"Um, Ms. Hunter, come in. Is everything okay? Thank you for giving me this opportunity. I know it won't last long but it is another tick in the box, isn't it?"

"Yes, it is."

Chase kept standing and looked at the stack of papers on the desk.

"I'm trying to go through all this and frankly it is a mess," Dustin offered.

"In what way? Chase moved closer to the desk to get a look at the paper Dustin was reading.

"Basically it is the filing system or lack of. I don't seem to see any kind of organization."

"Ross was unorganized?" The statement perplexed Chase. "I don't recall ever hearing anything like that. I know he did all the collection of data and put it all together for presentations and that would call for someone who is organized."

"That's just it…there was never a hint of disorganization. His team tells me that he knew all aspects of every project they did so I find this puzzling. It is almost like the papers were shuffled and dropped in a pile."

Chase knew a guard was with him when he emptied his office on Sunday. *But what about Friday before he left?* She knew he handed in his keycard so he couldn't get back in the building on Saturday. "Is that what you think happened, Mr. Stewart?"

Dustin shrugged. "It's the only answer I can think of."

"What are you going to do about it?'

"Sort through everything. I thought I'd get the team together in one of the conference rooms and see if we can make some sense out of these papers together. They would be more familiar with them than I'd be."

Chase smiled. "Excellent idea. Please let me know when you get it all straightened out so I can assign you and the team a new project."

"Will do." Dustin looked directly at Chase. "Ms. Hunter?"

"Yes."

"Do you mind my asking why Mr. Ross resigned?"

Chase considered the question, biting her lower lip as she thought. "Will you report what I tell you about it accurately?"

"Of course."

"You must share the information with the team and instruct them if they hear another version they must correct it immediately." Chase looked at the very good-looking young man with reddish blonde hair and raised an eyebrow.

"Yes, of course. Ever since I've worked here—four years now—each member of Mr. Ross' team has always been above board and never once did I hear anyone gossip."

Chase nodded then cleared her throat. "Mr. Ross has been under scrutiny for some time now. He finally went too far. As you know, Mr. Stewart, Eastman has a zero tolerance when it comes to sexual harassment. Mr. Ross gave us no choice and Mr. Eastman demanded his resignation."

Dustin's eyes were wide. "Some of the females on his team told me that they felt uncomfortable around him."

"If you hear anything like that again you must come to me or HR immediately. We cannot let the name of Eastman be tainted by such actions."

"I will."

"Excellent. Until we name a permanent manager, you will report directly to me. If you have any questions, no matter how insignificant you think they are, bring them to me."

Dustin held out his hand. "Again, thank you for giving me this opportunity and trusting me with the truth. I won't let you down."

Chase gave the man a firm handshake. "We will talk again next week unless a problem arises."

✝

Chase was pleased with her interaction with Dustin Stewart. *He would be an excellent candidate for the manager position, she thought. Unfortunately, there is only one position open.* As she walked to the other end of the corridor, she envisioned Becca in the plum colored suit she'd worn to work today. The closer Chase got to the office, where she knew she'd find Becca, the more her body reacted on a primal level.

She grinned. *Spontaneous combustion...what would the gossipmongers say then?*

Standing in front of Becca's door, Chase saw Becca sitting at the desk with her right hand fingers splayed through her auburn hair, her thumb resting on her cheek. She tapped a pen softly with her left hand.

Chase stood and watched her, heart swelling with tender feelings that she never thought she'd feel. *I should run away as fast as I can.* But her heart refused to let her. Chase knew, in that moment, she wanted Becca in her life for all time. She softly tapped the doorframe and saw Becca grin.

"Good morning, Ms. Hunter." A wide smile tugged Becca's lips. "I didn't know you made office calls."

"On special occasions I do." Chase took a step inside the door and stopped. "How are things going for you? Any snide comments or gestures?"

"I held a team meeting first thing this morning and explained that Mr. Douglas was no longer our manager and that he'd be taking another managerial position within the company." Becca shrugged. "They all seemed relieved. Their comments about Mr. Douglas were mostly derogatory in nature, especially about him taking all the accolades for their hard work. They were all very impressed by what you said about them at this past Thursday's get together." Becca smiled. "One of them said you are a class act and they all agreed."

"What about others outside of your team? Any problems?"

"Honestly, Chase, I didn't pay attention to anyone else. I'm busy figuring out Mr. Douglas's filing system and helping the team with the new project."

"Seems to be a common theme."

"I'm sorry?" Becca replied.

"Nothing important. Why not use his office?"

"I would feel funny being in his office with all his personal belongings. I will go in there only when I need to.

"Is it too much for you?" Chase looked at Becca with a worried expression.

"No, not at all. It is just that he never allowed me to be privy to any of this aspect. My role and the team's role were to make him look good."

"Just so you know, everyone knew who was responsible for his successes." Chase repressed the urge to go all the way inside the office, close the door, and lock it along with closing the blinds.

"Can you come in and have a seat?" Becca seemed to be reading her thoughts.

"No."

Becca frowned. "Why?'

"Because it isn't safe," Chase whispered as she looked to see if anyone was nearby. "I spoke with Edward Eastman and he has no problem with us dating as long as it doesn't interfere with our work. If I came any closer we'd be definitely interfering with work."

"You told him about us?"

"Yes. He's known for some time now that I am a lesbian and I wanted him to know that you and I are dating so everything is above board."

Becca let out a long sigh. "That was quite a chance you took. What if he said that he didn't approve."

Chase shrugged. "Then I'd be looking for a new job."

Becca stood and placed both palms on the desk. "No. I wouldn't let you do that."

"Darlin', the choice is not yours." Chase moved farther in the office, put her hands on the desk, and leaned in so that she was breathing the same air as Becca. "I've spent my whole life in the pursuit of being the best at everything. At a cost of having, no life of my own, and I don't want to live like that anymore. Especially…"

Becca grinned. "Especially what?"

"Since you've come into my life."

With a shrug, Becca moved back. "You know nothing about me, Chase. There are things that if you knew, you'd be repulsed and run for the hills."

"I know what I feel here." Chase tapped her heart. "There is nothing you could tell me that would make me…." She smiled. "*Run for the hills.*"

Voices from the hallway drifted toward them, Becca took her seat, and Chase moved several steps away.

"Have dinner with me tonight," Chase whispered.

"I can't. There's no one to let Georgie out." Becca folded her hands in front of her, as the voices grew closer.

"I passed a little diner on the way to your house. We could go there and you'd be almost home." Chase's eyes searched Becca's. "Come on…say *yes*. I hear they have a kickass meatloaf."

Becca laughed. "You're too funny."

"I'll take that as a *yes*." Chase heard the voices outside the door. "Please let me know, Ms. Cameron if you need help on anything else."

She turned to the door and smiled at Joyce Westcott and Randy Archer who were standing there.

"Keep up the good work." Chase moved past the two, still smiling.

†

"Okay, come clean with it…how'd you know about the meatloaf?" Becca gave Chase a suspicious look. "Have you been here before?"

Chase laughed heartily. "No. It just stands to reason that a diner jam-packed with people waiting for seats could mean only one thing—excellent food."

Becca watched Chase as she spoke while waving her fork around the diner. "Do you know how glad I am that you came into my life?"

After putting her fork down, Chase reached across the small table and took Becca's hand. "I know exactly how you feel. It is like all my life I've been striving to succeed and every time I do, I tell myself no, *that isn't it*. And here you are sitting across from me and my mind and heart are telling me *this is it*."

Becca closed her eyes and sighed. "It is like you're reading my mind. It is so hard to believe how fast this is happening to us." She squeezed Chase's hand. "It is only about twenty minutes to my house. Do you want to come home with me?"

A wide grin crossed Chase's face. "How did you know I always travel with a change of clothes?"

"No. You don't. You're kidding me right."

"If you take me home, I'll show you." Chase wiggled her eyebrows. "That is if your invitation is serious about always being welcome in your home."

Becca picked up the check, put a twenty on the table, scraped her chair back, and winked at Chase. "You can follow me."

†

The watcher peered through the darkness at the house without lights on and the road absent of any car's headlights. It was already ten o'clock and for Becca to be away that long could only mean something was wrong. But the watcher didn't have the feeling that was the reason for Becca being late.

A glimpse of light from the dirt road caught the watcher's attention. When a second set of headlights appeared, the watcher grinned as hands clapped. "Yes, at last. It certainly has taken her long enough to find her soul mate."

The watcher saw Becca get out of her car and walk toward the woman exiting the other vehicle. They embraced and kissed before the woman opened her trunk and produced a bag. "You be good to her, Chase. She has waited a long time for you to come into her life so show her the proper respect."

With eyes closed, the watcher sent a whispered message into Chase's ear.

As if she heard the watcher's words, Chase turned her head toward the deer stand and nodded.

Chapter Fourteen

Georgette twisted, turned, and barked as Becca and Chase entered the house.

In her hand, Chase held a doggy bag that contained two pieces of meatloaf.

"Sit and be patient," Becca said.

Georgie sat and wagging her stubby tail.

"Apparently Georgie thinks I brought this for her," Chase mused. "Too bad she doesn't know I'm holding on to it in case there are no eggs in the morning."

"If you expect her to let you get near me, I'd suggest you give her what you have. I've seen her vengeful side and trust me, it isn't pretty."

Chase offered a lopsided grin as the two of them headed for the kitchen. "I should save this for the morning right?" She held up the bag.

"You can give her a taste now and we can refrigerate the rest until tomorrow morning." Becca opened the refrigerator door and smiled. "You're in luck. We have fresh eggs for the morning. Although it won't be as lavish as the last breakfast you last ate here, unless I get up early. Can't be late for work. The boss will frown if I do that."

"Says who? I'm the boss and I set the rules. You can come into work late if that is what is needed."

"What happened to not mixing business and pleasure?" Becca asked with a serious look on her face.

Chase searched Becca's face before finally resting her arms on the counter behind Becca. "Maybe I should go."

Becca's eyes grew wide and she looked crestfallen. "Why? Isn't this what you want…what we both want?"

Chase tugged Becca to her then engulfed her in her arms. "Becca, I am so ready for you that I think I will explode."

She kissed the top of her head. "The very first time I made love with a woman I thought it would last forever. Regina only wanted a quick fuck. Sorry to use that word but it is the only one that described what it was."

She hugged Becca closer.

"I was devastated and instead of socializing and perhaps meeting someone else, I threw myself into my studies. I vowed never to give my heart to another. Oh, there were others, none of which lasted very long and none of them touched my heart." Chase shrugged. "Ultimately my work became my lover."

"I'm so sorry to hear that, Chase."

"Don't be sorry because in the end, I'm the winner. I found you. I could kick myself for all the time I wasted just watching you and not making any contact. Never before, have I found complete peace. There isn't anything I wouldn't do for you, Becca. Nothing."

Becca was sobbing.

Chase tilted Becca's chin up so she could look into her eyes. "What's the matter? Why are you crying?"

"Because you make me feel the same way. I fear that once you find out what I did you will leave me." Becca swiped at the tears rolling down her cheek. "I don't want to lose you."

"Tell me and let me be the judge of how I will feel and not have you assign whether I leave or not."

Becca took Chase's hand and led her to the sofa where they sat in unison.

✝

The watcher's eyes closed while listening to the conversation and sent up a silent prayer. *Dear, Lord, please give Becca the courage to reveal what's in her heart. I am certain Chase won't leave her for she has a tender soul. Please hear my prayer and help this lost soul. Amen.*

✝

Becca was trembling as tears cascaded down her cheeks. "I…."

Chase hugged Becca so close that their bodies intertwined. "Nothing you can say will turn me away from you. Please believe that and trust in me."

With watery eyes, Becca nodded. "I do trust you."

"Then tell me what makes you so sad."

"Sad? Why would you say something like that?"

"I can see it in your eyes. There are times when you get this far away look and I can see the pain reflected in your eyes."

Becca snorted. "Didn't know I was that transparent."

She grabbed a tissue and blew her nose. "Okay, here goes. A year ago—August thirty-first so it is more like fourteen months—my mother asked me to change a light bulb in the kitchen. I said I would when I had the time."

Becca sucked in a cleansing breath.

"I remember we were in the middle of negotiations and Mr. Douglas was on my back constantly so I was so preoccupied with only one thing—the project. Funny. I don't even remember the name of the project. Anyway, my mom got tired of waiting for me, got the ladder out, and attempted to change the bulb herself. She was eighty-three years old and vibrant even though she'd had several bouts with dizziness and falling down."

Becca looked down, shook her head, and became silent.

It wasn't hard for Chase to figure out what happened but she knew Becca needed to tell the entire story.

"What happened next?" Chase kissed Becca's cheek. "I'm right here and I'm not going anywhere."

Becca looked directly at Chase. "For now."

"Forever."

Becca sighed. "I came in late that night and found my mother on the floor, the ladder lying next to her. Georgie was lying by her side with her head on Mom's shoulder. I thought she must have had a dizzy spell and fell off the ladder. I have no idea how long she laid there alone and most likely terrified. The fact that she hadn't started dinner and that her body was cold told me she'd been there for quite some time."

"Was there an autopsy done?"

With a nod, Becca's tears renewed. "They said she had a stroke and probably died instantly." Becca lifted one shoulder. "I'm certain that the fall is what killed her and it was my fault. Had she not been on that ladder she might have been able to call for help...." Becca's eyes grew distant. "If I'd only changed that stupid light bulb when she asked, I know she would still be here today. I killed my mother as if I put a gun to her head and shot her dead."

Chase made no further comment and just held Becca tight. Once Becca's crying slowed, Chase stood and took Becca's hand. "Come with me. You need to go to bed and get a good night's sleep."

"Will you stay with me and hold me," Becca asked in a soft pleading voice.

"For as long as you want me too. Come on, it is getting late."

Chase helped Becca undress and marveled at Becca's body. She was trim and her breasts were the perfect size for her body.

She's more exquisite than I ever imagined, she thought.

She wanted Becca and silently groaned as she covered that body with an oversized T-shirt. *Not tonight.*

Becca slipped under the covers and patted the bed beside her. "Sleep here."

"Okay." Chase took off her own clothes, slid next to Becca and put an arm around her.

"Hey, you're naked. I'm sorry this night didn't go the way we'd planned."

"It was a perfect night. You needed to tell me what was eating at you so we can move forward. There is plenty of time for the physical."

"I'll make it up to you, I promise."

Chase drew Becca near. "You trusted me with your deepest darkest secret and I hope you can find peace now."

"You're still here and that gives me peace." Becca yawned and in a few seconds was sound asleep.

"Sleep well, my darling. I will be here protecting you throughout the night." Chase yawned and kissed the back of Becca's head before she too fell into a deep sleep.

†

The watcher clapped in delight.

"I can't wait to get home."

Secure in the knowledge that Becca was safe and loved, the watcher climbed down the ladder before walking at a fast pace down the narrow deer path.

"This has been the best night since I started watching out for Becca." A wide grin formed on the watcher's face. "Life is good."

†

Becca stretched and smiled, feeling the arm around her. Chase stayed. *She heard what I'd done and she's still here.* Chase moved and drew her closer making Becca close her eyes and purr.

"Good morning."

Chase's deep, sensuous voice sent a harsh primal need coursing through Becca's body.

"Good morning. Thanks for being here."

"Please turn so I can see your face." Chase lifted her arm so Becca could turn and face her. "Yep, you're just as beautiful first thing in the morning."

"And you, Ms. Hunter are naked and in my bed. Whatever should I do about that?"

Chase pinched the sleeve of Becca's shirt. "This should come off."

"First I need to use the bathroom and brush my teeth."

Becca moved off the bed as Chase reached for her. From the bathroom, Becca watched in fascination as Chase pushed the covers back and moved toward the bathroom.

"Me too. You can't have clean breath when my teeth…" She ran her tongue across her teeth. "Feel like they have little jackets on."

Becca opened the medicine cabinet door and grabbed a new toothbrush. "Here you go. I'll meet you back in bed."

"You got that right. Thanks." Chase held up the toothbrush.

Becca was lying in the bed naked with all the covers pushed away when Chase walked into the bedroom, Becca smiled seductively as her eyes raked across the beautiful supple body. Becca held out a hand. "Join me."

It didn't take long before their bodies touched. "We're a perfect fit aren't we," Chase whispered. "I've dreamt about being with you just like this. It's hard to believe it's really you."

"I am real and I am where I want…no…need to be." Becca brushed the hair away from Chase's face. "You stayed."

"Of course I did. You are where I need to be. Pinch me and let me know this is real."

Becca obliged.

"Ow. Yep, we are real." Chase's lips brushed Becca's before kissing her deeply. "I want you so much."

Becca said nothing as she kissed Chase again as her finger slowly made its way down to the valley between Chase's breasts. As the kisses heated, Becca swirled her finger around a hard, erect nipple before pinching it lightly.

Chase groaned. "Please, don't stop."

"I have no intention of stopping." Becca's lips curved around one hardened nipple and her fingers pulled gently on the other one. When Chase's hand held her head in place, Becca nipped the nipple with her teeth.

Chase moaned long and hard. "Oh, God, I never imagined this."

Chase was breathing fast and hard when Becca's fingers finally slid down her belly, past her belly button, and along her wet center.

Becca teased Chase, for what seemed like hours, by entering her and pumping gently then removing all contact. She pulled back and looked at the pleasure radiating from Chase's face.

"You are so beautiful."

Becca kissed Chase then pulled back and smiled before her lips followed the journey of her fingers. There was no doubt that Chase was well on her way to orgasm and Becca wanted their first time to be special. Her fingers began moving rhythmically as her lips tugged at Chase's clitoris before lavishing it with her tongue. Becca could feel a tightening around her fingers and she slipped in one more finger seconds before Chase lifted off the bed and cried out.

Chase, panting hard, looked at Becca who was still between her legs, lovingly kissing her thighs. "That was the most amazing orgasm. Come up here so I can kiss you."

Becca kissed her way up Chase's body. She licked her lips before kissing her. "Can you taste how delectable you are?"

"Oh, yes." Chase flipped Becca easily. "Now be ready for me to devour you." A wicked grin crossed her face as a finger slipped through Becca's drenched folds.

With an urgency that Becca had never known existed, she welcomed every one of Chase's advances, encouraging her to take all of her.

†

Two hours later, both women's bodies remained intertwined as they murmured words of the passion they just shared. It wasn't until Chase's phone rang that they even noticed what time it was.

"Damn, that's Debra's ring tone." Chase got out of bed and began searching in her pile of clothing until she found the phone. "Hunter… yes, Debra, I am well aware of the time… something came up that needed my immediate attention… that is not all that urgent. Just call and reschedule for this afternoon… yes, I will call you when I'm on my way in."

Chase winked at Becca and grinned. "In all my years with Eastman I've never been late. Yet you, my little vixen, make me want to stay right here with you forever."

Becca slipped out of bed and wrapped her arms around Chase. "A vixen, am I? Then you are the hunter. Good thing I want you to catch me."

She took Chase's hand. "Come on we need to shower and at least get to work before noon. I can only imagine what the gossip will be when I am not at work on time."

Chase laughed. "You? The last time I didn't come to work it was when I had the flu and stayed home for two days. Debra called me constantly to make sure I was doing okay and to update me on what was happening at work." Chase grinned. "I like making love with you as my reason for being late."

✝

Drinking her coffee and munching on toast, Chase looked at Becca. "Tell me about your parents."

Becca's eyebrows knitted. "Why?"

"I'm interested. Please tell me a memory you have of your dad."

With a smile, Becca nodded. "He was the salt of the earth. I remember one Christmas when he volunteered to take food and clothing that the church had collected to a needy family."

Becca took in a deep breath. "I remember it was freezing and snow was everywhere. When we got there the father of the family came out to help carry in the stuff. The man had on a tattered shirt, threadbare jeans, and tennis shoes. My dad told him it was too cold to be out without a coat and gloves and the man said he didn't have any."

A smile crossed Becca's face. "My dad took off his coat and gloves and gave them to the man. When we saw his wife appear, dad nudged me, and I took off my coat and gloves. He literally gave that man the shirt off his back. On the ride back I asked him why and he told me that we were fortunate to have other coats and gloves, that not everyone did and we had to always remember that."

"That is an awesome memory," Chase said. "What about your mom?"

"My mom was the type of person who would make sure she visited anyone in need. She had a pot of soup on the stove constantly just in case someone was ill and needed her chicken soup."

Becca looked out the window. "I remember her taking me with her to visit an elderly woman who was house bound. We'd buy groceries, go there, clean her house, and make sure she had something hot to eat. She told me it was how we treated others that would leave an indelible mark on the world."

Becca rubbed a finger over her tear-filled eyes. "My indelible mark will be that I wasn't there when she needed me the most."

Chase knelt by Becca's chair and taking her hand, she kissed it tenderly. "Becca, by remembering our loved ones who have passed they continue to live here." She touched the skin above Becca's heart. "A blood clot was the cause of your mother's death and not your negligence in changing a light bulb."

"I know but it hurts so much."

"Instead of thinking about your mom and the light bulb, let your mind fill with all those happy moments you shared with her."

"It can't be that simple."

"It is that simple." Chase stood and pulled Becca up with her. "Just give it a try for me. Okay?"

Becca buried her face in Chase's should. "For you, I will."

The kisses they shared were tender and loving. Becca moved away first. "We need to get to work and you kissing me like that makes it very difficult to let you go."

Chase's phone rang. "It's Debra again." Her arm encircled Becca's waist.

"Debra, I am getting ready to leave now... I will be in the office in about an hour."

Chapter Fifteen

Becca gave Chase a fifteen-minute lead before she started the long drive into the city. She was still basking in the glow of their lovemaking. Chase was so loving and tender that Becca found herself sinking into her lover, as they became one. It was a feeling so overwhelming that Becca craved Chase as if she were a drug.

Her phone rang and Becca smiled, expecting it to be Chase. Becca's eyes widened when she heard the static and someone calling her name. This time the voice was a bit clearer… *Becca, I need you.* "Who is this and why do you keep calling me?"

She listened intently but all she heard was louder static so she disconnected. "Arrgh…these calls are maddening."

Becca's phone rang again and she looked at the name—it was Chase and pushed the Bluetooth button.

"Hi beautiful. Want to turn around and play hooky with me today?"

Chase let out a rich laugh. "As tempting as that is I need to attend the monthly staff meeting at one-thirty."

"Oh."

"Hey, don't sound so sad. We have the rest of our lives," Chase said softly.

"Tonight then?" Becca shook her head. *I sound so pathetic.* "Sorry I was just thinking about you and I'm missing you. I know you have a life outside of work."

"Becca, what is going on? Why are you upset?"

Becca bit the inside of her cheek in an attempt to hold it together. "I'm not upset, Chase. Emotions that I never thought I'd feel are making me feel vulnerable. I know that once I get to work, I will need to put all thoughts of you and this morning behind me and do my job."

"You're not the only one who is feeling vulnerable. The temptation to chuck it all and go back to your home is overwhelming and I am trying hard to keep going toward Eastman."

"I know," Becca whispered. "We will work something out."

"Yes, we will. We've both waited too long to find one another and now that we have, I am not letting you go."

Becca heard Chase's voice soft and full of emotion. "Nor am I going to let you go." She smiled. "You are going into the parking lot aren't you?"

"Yep, and now I'm heading for my parking spot then I'll go inside to a dull meeting. On the upside, I can sit there recalling your body next to mine."

"Stop." Becca grinned. "If you keep talking like that I won't be responsible if I come to your office and lock the door."

"Is that a promise?"

"Yes."

"Listen, babe, I need to go or I *will* be late. I'll call you later."

"Okay, have a great day."

"Already did, darling."

Becca could hear the laughter in Chase's voice as she hung up and she chuckled.

✝

A light knock on the doorframe of her office door made Becca look up. The moment she saw Kim standing there, she felt disappointed that it wasn't Chase.

"Hi, Bec, are you okay?"

"Why wouldn't I be?" Becca tried to keep herself in check and not be rude to her friend.

"Because you didn't come into work until after the noon hour." Kim moved farther into the office. "I've never known you to do that. What's going on?"

Becca pondered how much to tell her. Kim was her friend but she wanted to keep Chase private. "I was overwhelmed last night with memories of my mom."

"Oh, sweetie, why? What happened to bring you back to those recollections?"

Becca shook her head. "It was time to put the past where it belongs."

"And, how do you feel about that?"

"I finally came to the realization that mom had a stroke and falling off the ladder didn't kill her, the stroke did. I was working so there was no way I could have been there for her. My only regret now is that she died alone."

"But she didn't, Bec. She had Georgie with her. I remember you telling me that when you found her Georgie was resting her head on your mom's shoulder."

Becca let a genuine smile cross her face. "That is true. I hadn't thought of it as that. Thank you, Kim, for reminding me of that."

Becca felt the remnants of grief that had burdened her heart for more than a year lift.

"So I take it you had a hard time sleeping and that is why you were late," Kim said with affection. "You should have called me and I would have helped you through the torment your heart was feeling."

"It was something I needed to do by myself."

Becca didn't like evading the truth but until things between her and Chase solidified, she had to keep their bourgeoning relationship to herself. It was bad enough that she told Kim about Chase in the first place.

Kim came around the desk and gave Becca a hug. "I love you. You do know that right?"

"I do, I'm sorry it didn't work out between us. It was all me. You are a wonderful friend to me and I am fortunate that you are still in my life."

"Want to go to dinner with me tonight?"

Becca shook her head. "Not tonight, I am exhausted and all I want is to have a glass of wine and crawl into bed." She saw the defeated look on Kim's face. "I'm sorry, Kim. It's not personal. I just don't have anything left today to be a decent dinner companion."

"Maybe another time."

"Count on it. I promise."

Kim gave Becca another quick hug and smiled at her. "I will be looking forward to it."

After Kim left, Becca pushed the back of the chair to a semi-reclining position. She closed her eyes and envisioned Chase making love with her. Becca smiled as her body reacted to the memory.

The ringing of the phone woke Becca just as she dozed. "This is Becca Cameron, how may I help you."

"You sound wonderful. I just wanted to hear your voice."

"Where are you?"

"Between meetings. Unfortunately I have to go to a dinner with our out of town top echelon colleagues."

Becca said nothing even as her eyes watered.

"If it helps, I'd rather spend the night with you."

Becca could hear the sincerity in Chase's voice. "I know. I still can be disappointed can't I?"

"Believe me when I say that I am as disappointed as you are. I've thought of nothing else but you." Chase laughed. "One of the other VP's was droning on and on about something ridiculous and he asked me a question."

"Oh, no you didn't." Becca giggled.

"Yep, I just looked at him with what I am sure was a blank look and told him I didn't understand the question and could he repeat it."

"Did he buy it?"

"Apparently so. He asked the question again and just as I was about to answer he changed the subject."

Chase let out a long sigh. "I'm sorry but I have to go. Hopefully we can get together tomorrow."

"Okay. I'll be looking forward to it."

"I've cleared my calendar of anything after three in the afternoon."

Becca smiled. "I miss you. Be careful out there. I don't know what I'd do if I lost you after just finding you."

"Is it okay to call you when I get home, Becca?"

"I'd like that."

"I will then. Sorry, I am already late."

The phone disconnected before Becca had a chance to say goodbye.

Becca looked at the phone and nodded. "I know what I have to do."

She moved her mouse, opened a blank word document, and typed.

✝

For Becca the ride home that day seemed to take forever. When she passed under the flashing light, she smiled, knowing she'd be home in ten or fifteen minutes. Becca's truck hadn't gone but a mile past when her phone rang. She looked at the time. *Is she done already?*

"Hey if I'd known you were going to be home this early I would have stayed—"

Static and crackling on the other end had Becca ready to hang up. Then she listened and the words she heard were as clear as a bell. *Please come to me, Becca.* A chill ran up her spine as the voice disappeared into the static.

"What the hell is this all about?" Becca pushed on the gas pedal and drove as fast as she could until she came to the road leading to her house. The voice had spooked her and her only thought was to get inside her home and lock the doors.

✝

"It was so odd, Chase. Static then a very clear voice said *come to me, Becca.* It scared the bejesus out of me." Becca pressed the speaker setting.

"Do you want me to drive out and stay with you?"

"As tempting as that offer sounds, it is already eight-thirty, and if you came out we'd not get to work on time again. Besides, it is so dark out tonight that I'd worry the whole time you were on the road. I've got the alarm set and Georgie is here to warn me if anything is amiss."

"Are you sure?"

"Yes."

"Was the voice male or female?" Chase asked.

Becca thought for a moment. "Actually it was a neutral sounding voice. I don't think I could call it either gender."

"That is just plain weird, Becca. You know I won't sleep a wink worrying about you so you should let me come out there."

"No, and not because I don't want you to…believe me I do. Last night when I told you about my mom and how she died, along with our discussion this morning, it was like a catharsis for me. You helped me lift the burden of guilt and shame and to see things as how they were and not how I interpreted them. Now that I have you in my life it is such an overwhelming sensation that I need to sort it all out." Becca gnawed at her lip. "Does that make sense at all?"

"Yes, sweetheart, it makes perfect sense." It took a few seconds for Chase to continue. "Promise me that you will be safe and if anything strange happens you will call the police and then me."

"I promise. Good night, Chase. Sleep well."

"You too. I will see you in the morning."

✝

The watcher listened to the conversation between the two women and frowned the entire time.

I told them it was too soon to make contact. All they've done now is to scare her and that isn't what we want.

With a decision made, the watcher hunkered down in the subzero-sleeping bag.

I can't let Becca be alone tonight. She's too fragile and if I must, I will comfort her if she cries out in the night. Idiots. We were so close. Now it will be up to me to repair the damage.

The watcher growled and pulled the sleeping bag close. It was a cold dark night and there was no telling what might be lurking about in Becca's mind.

I'll have to come up with another type of concoction that will keep the nightmares they will cause away.

✝

Surprised at how refreshed she felt, Becca gave Georgie a quick pat along with a rawhide bone before leaving the house. Becca got in her truck and once she left her dirt road, she picked up speed. She was eager to catch

153

Chase before the day began. After Becca parked, she grabbed her cell phone from the seat and smiled. There hadn't been any strange calls. *At least that's one less worry…I hope.*

She quickly exited her truck and walked with purpose toward the Eastman building noticing that Chase's car was already there. She began dialing Chase's number only to stop.

It's still early and judging by the parking lot, not many people are here yet. I'll surprise her.

Becca grinned envisioning the look on Chase's face.

Chapter Sixteen

The elevator stopped at the eighteenth floor and Becca was relieved to see that Debra wasn't there yet. She was desperate to see Chase, walked quickly toward her office, and rapped lightly on the door.

"Come in."

Becca shivered at the low sexy sound of Chase's voice. She opened the door and saw Chase sitting behind her desk with Debra and a man Becca did not know standing in front of the desk. She gulped.

Shit, think of something plausible to say.

The feeling of the blush beginning on her face made her want to run and hide. "Oh, I'm sorry to bother you, Ms. Hunter. I have a question about the new project you assigned my team. I'd hoped to catch you before your day began but I see that I was wrong. I will email you about the problem."

Becca's eyes darted to the man then to Debra, and finally they fell on Chase. "That's what I should have done in the first place. Again, I'm sorry to have interrupted."

Becca knew she was babbling as all eyes turned to look at her.

Chase grinned. "Ms. Cameron, if you will have a seat in the waiting area, I will see you as soon as I am done here. It shouldn't be long."

Becca took a step back and pulled the door closed.

Becca rapidly made her way to the waiting area where she sat before burying her face in her hands. *What an idiot I am! I should have called first. Stupid, stupid, stupid.*

"Ms. Cameron, are you okay," Debra asked, entering the waiting area.

Becca looked up and gave the woman a crooked smile. "Yes, I should have called first and not embarrassed myself that way."

"Ms. Hunter will see you now. Make it short, okay? She has a breakfast meeting in fifteen minutes."

Debra sounded vexed and Becca debated whether to go in and see Chase or just go down to her own office.

"Is there a problem?" Debra asked.

Becca pushed off the chair and stood. "No. None at all."

✝

After hearing Chase call *come in*, Becca opened the door and began talking immediately. "I'm so sorry. I am mortified, interrupting you like that."

"Do you know how cute you are when you blush?" Chase chuckled. "You didn't interrupt anything. I was hurrying them along so I could call you and see if you are free for lunch."

"Really? That's amazing. I was going to ask you the same thing."

"Great minds think alike. Now," Chase took Becca in her arms. "How about a good morning kiss."

Their kiss was long and passionate, full of promises of what was yet to come. Both Becca and Chase caught up in the glory of the kiss they didn't hear the phone ringing. It wasn't until someone knocked on the door that Becca broke away from Chase.

Chase moved toward her desk and Becca followed but not too close behind.

Another knock sounded. Chase growled. "Come in."

Debra opened the door. "The breakfast meeting starts in two minutes. If you leave now you will just make it."

Chase narrowed her eyes. "I will see you later about that problem, Ms. Cameron. Will you text me a time when you're available?"

Becca nodded. "Certainly." She moved past Debra and caught a cold glare coming from the woman. As she was closing the door, she heard Chase's business voice.

"Never again interrupt me when I am in a meeting with one of my managers. When you come into my office to remind me of a meeting or such it makes me look like I'm a little child that you are reprimanding like a mother. Don't you ever do that again. As for being late, I have been to these meetings and I know how things work. They won't be starting for at least another fifteen minutes."

"I'm sorry," Debra said. "But you asked…."

Becca heard no more as the door clicked shut and she made her way to the elevators. She was almost to the elevator when she heard Debra call out to her.

"Wait," Debra's voice commanded.

Becca entered the elevator and pushed the close button before Debra came into view. *I can only imagine what she wanted to tell me. Something like keep away from her or you'll be sorry. I wonder if she has a thing for Chase.*

When the chime sounded for her floor, Becca exited and went straight to her office. Her lips were still tingling from the passionate kiss Chase had given her.

✝

The rest of the day was crazy with demands on both Chase and Becca. The lunch they planned on sharing never happened when Chase found out that all the VP's were responsible for taking the clients to lunch. Chase made a quick stop by Becca's office to explain why lunch wasn't going to happen for them.

"Hi, give me a minute to collect my lunch and then I'll be ready to go." Becca grinned.

"I'm sorry but I can't have lunch with you today." Chase saw the disappointment without Becca saying a word. "If it helps, they leave early tomorrow morning and all obligations will be gone."

"Is that a promise?" Becca asked.

"You can count on it. We will have a date tomorrow evening. That I promise. If it means I get reprimanded for not doing something, it will be worth it to have you all to myself."

"I thought we weren't going to do anything that would jeopardize our jobs."

"I won't but, if it comes down to not seeing you tomorrow night and being here, you win every time."

"Like today?"

"Ouch."

"I'm sorry, Chase. I'm being a bitch and you don't deserve my snide comments." She sighed. "It's been a long day that started out with me making a fool of myself in front of your staff." Becca blew out an audible breath. "I'm sorry about that."

"Seeing you standing in the doorway was the brightest spot in my day other than the electrifying kiss we shared."

"For me too." Becca leaned back in her chair. "You'd better go or Debra will find you and remind you of your obligations. I think she has a crush on you."

Chase laughed. "She is happily married with two kids. It's more like she is protective of me. Remember I told you she always tries hooking me up with women."

"I will never do anything to hurt you, Chase."

Chase pushed the door closed. "Come here," she whispered. "I need to feel your body next to mine."

No sooner had Becca pushed her chair back and stood that there was a knock on the door. "Dammit," she whispered. "We can't get a break can we?'

In a graceful turn, Chase opened the door. "Hello, Randy, it's good to see you again. How are things coming along with the new project?"

Randy Archer's eyes darted between Becca and the VP. "There are a few glitches we need to work out before we do our first walk through of the company."

"Excellent. Keep up the good work." Chase patted the man's shoulder. "We will continue this discussion later, Ms. Cameron." Chase looked at her wristwatch. "Unfortunately, I have a lunch meeting to attend." With those words, Chase smiled at Becca before leaving the office."

"What is it, Randy?" Becca asked.

†

The rest of the day dragged by, Becca fielding questions from the team about what to do with certain information about the company they were investigating for possible purchase. Before she knew it, it was six-thirty and she hadn't heard anything from Chase.

Guess she got too involved to even text me. Becca couldn't keep the resentment out of her thoughts. When she was with Kim, she had always put her job and family first before thinking about Kim.

"Guess it is payback time," she said aloud.

Becca left the building, pressed the automatic start button, and unlocked her truck. The air was frosty and made her skin feel cold. She thought back to the weekend when Chase's warm hand pressed against her cheek. "God, I'm acting like some lovesick puppy."

Just like the day, the drive home seemed longer to Becca than usual. As she got to the flashing yellow light, her phone rang and she pressed the Bluetooth connection hoping it wasn't the static crap again. "Hello," she said in the coldest voice she could.

"Shall I call back or just go away?" Chase asked.

"Crap, I'm sorry. I thought it was the static I always get when the phone rings while I'm driving this stretch of the road."

"Can't you look at the screen and see the readout of who is calling?"

"I don't like to take my eyes off the road. It has to do with the deer thing. I never want to be up close and personal with them again."

"Ah. Would you rather I hang up so you can concentrate on driving."

"No," Becca whispered. "Hearing your voice is the best thing that's happened to me since we met briefly before lunch." She shrugged. "Please don't go. I'm sorry once again for being a bitch."

"Sounds more like stressed out than a bitch. I just wish I could have been there for you yesterday and today."

"It's the job, Chase. If anyone understands that, it's me. Besides, we are taking it slow right?"

"Yes, we did agree to that. Just for the record, I'd rather have been with you than at work and to be honest that scares me."

"Why?'

"Because work has been my life for so long that I can't believe how easy it is for me to make the transition to having you in my life." There were a few seconds of silence. "I am so happy that we found one another," she whispered.

"So am I." Becca smiled as she turned down her dirt road. "I'm almost to my house. Can I call you back in about ten minutes?"

"I wish. I am hiding in the bathroom so I could call you. The final function is in full swing and all I want is to be with you."

"Do what you have to, Chase. I'm not going anywhere." Becca smiled knowing she meant every word.

"That's all I needed to know. In case you were wondering, I'm not going anywhere either."

Becca could hear the sincerity in Chase's voice. "Just don't forget that tomorrow you are mine and I don't like sharing."

Chase laughed. "Neither do I. Expect to see me waiting in your office tomorrow morning. We will lock the door and close the blinds."

"I like the sound of that."

"Good. Keep that thought. Now, I need to go mingle and be personable."

"Good bye, Chase. I'll look forward to tomorrow."

"Me too, bye."

✝

The watcher kept an eye on Becca as she sat in her truck for some time after pulling into the shed. *I wonder what she's doing.* The watcher was certain that Becca hadn't received any unexplained phone calls.

When Becca finally exited the truck and went inside her house, the watcher pressed a finger against the earpiece of the listening device. As she did every day, Becca turned off the alarm and spoke to Georgie. "How are you doing, girl. Burr, it's cold in here. What do you say we get a fire going and then have some supper? Soup will be good, I think."

She sounds okay. The watcher had heard Becca's voice so often that tinges of sadness came across loud and clear. *Why are you sad?*

The watcher's mind went blank and opened itself to the universe searching for Chase Hunter. When the watcher found the woman who was at a company function, the implementation of a deep mind probe began. Just as expected, Chase's mind focused on Becca. What was happening around her was of no concern to Chase.

The watcher took a deep breath as the present swirled all around again. "So why are you still sad, Becca," the watcher whispered.

Tomorrow I will change the sachet to a different mixture that will help her be happier. The watcher grinned. *Compared to a few weeks ago she is giddy and it is all because she found her soul mate.*

Sometime later, Becca's voice boomed in the earpiece and the watcher knew she must be right by the device.

"You know, Georgie, I'm smitten with my boss. Whatever am I going to do? I can't walk past her without wanting to take her in my arms and never letting her go." Becca laughed. "She's brought me out of the darkness. It's happening so fast it's a blur that but I know in my heart how right it feels. Come on, girl, I'll let you out one more time then we will go to bed after I wash my soup bowl and spoon. I have a big day ahead of me."

The watcher's hands clapped. *Now I must move forward with great caution. There can be no more mistakes like yesterday. Patience is needed until it is revelation time.*

When all the lights went out in Becca's house, the watcher climbed down the ladder with a lighter heart and followed the narrow path home.

Chapter Seventeen

Becca looked herself up and down in the full-length mirror in the bathroom. She had on her best suit—a black Gucci jacket along with a matching skirt and a silk cream-colored shell. Tonight she and Chase were going out on a date and she wanted to look her best. She chose a pair of black pumps to finish off the look.

"Wonder what she will be wearing." Her hand flew to her mouth. "What if I am overdressed?"

She thought back to how Chase dressed for work and concluded that how she was dressed was exactly Chase's attire.

"Right, this is it then." She drew a finger of Chanel behind each ear and between her breasts. "I'll take the bottle with me for a touch up just before we meet for dinner."

Satisfied with her look and that she had everything she needed, Becca dashed off a quick note to Gwen. *Gwen, I may be coming home later than usual tonight. Will you please let Georgie out one last time before you leave and make sure she has food and water? Thanks, Becca.*

Becca's mind wondered as she drove into work. Chase had told her she'd be waiting in her office when she got there and that made Becca smile. "I wonder if she meant it about locking the door and closing the blinds."

She could feel her body react to the sensuous thoughts that Chase always made her feel. Becca craved Chase's touch much as she thought an addict craved drugs or alcohol. The closer she got to work and her office the more aroused she became.

Becca shook her head and turned up the radio. "How am I going to get through this day? I'd better hole myself up in my office so I don't pass out from my thoughts of Chase."

†

With great anticipation, Becca unlocked her door and peered inside. Chase was sitting on her desk with her legs crossed at the ankles. Becca closed her eyes as she felt a tremor of an orgasm form. Returning her gaze to Chase, she pushed the door shut and locked it. "I've been thinking of this moment all morning," Becca said as she moved toward Chase.

Chase grinned. "Will you show me how much?"

Becca nodded and put her arms around Chase before gently touching her lips to Chase's mouth. "Are there any meetings you are scheduled for today?"

"My calendar is clear. What about you?"

"The only name on my calendar is yours." Becca's kisses were feather light on Chase's neck. Her lips moved down to the valley of Chase's breasts. "I want you and I don't want to wait."

"Me either. I have a plan."

"Really? Does it revolve around how wet I am for you?"

"Most definitely."

"Do tell me your plan because I don't think I can hold out much longer."

Chase slipped off the desk. "I think you and I should go on a field trip."

"That sounds interesting."

"Oh, it is, I promise you that. I've already made all the arrangements. So if you will please come with me, we shall get started."

"Are we going to look at a building?"

"Yes."

"One that Eastman is going to acquire?"

"No."

"Then where?"

"My apartment."

Becca grinned. "I like the way your mind works. I am looking forward to inspecting the property thoroughly."

Chase gave Becca a kiss so full of promise that Becca groaned as she felt her arousal building.

"We'd better hurry before I take you here," Becca promised.

✝

Becca pulled her truck next to Chase's BMW in the parking garage for one of the city's most upscale apartments. She couldn't concentrate on where she was for all she wanted was Chase in her arms.

Chase exited her vehicle and was by Becca's side within seconds. She grabbed Becca's hand and led her quickly to the elevator. "My place is on the tenth floor."

A keycard slid into a slot, the door opened immediately and they entered. Chase pushed a button, and the elevator began its ascent. The sexual energy was palpable as Chase and Becca stood close together, holding hands.

Once the elevator stopped on the tenth floor, Chase took Becca's hand and walked at a quick pace toward her apartment door. She fumbled with the key and snarled before it finally opened.

Without words, Chase pulled Becca to her and kissed her passionately. She grasped at the jacket Becca was wearing and tugged it off before pulling the silk shell off Becca as a trail of clothes led to the bedroom.

Chase growled. "I've been dreaming of making love with you my every waking moment."

Becca put her hands on Chase's cheeks then pulled her close. "Kiss me."

With their bodies entwined, fingers, lips, and tongues told the story of passion, sensuality and devotion. Throughout the day they made love that was at first full of hunger then led to gentle passion. Their souls clung together as the promise of a life together passed between them.

Becca rested her head on Chase's shoulder and sighed in satisfaction. "I never dreamed that making love could be so wondrous. And, had someone told me a few weeks ago that I'd be playing hooky with you on a weekday I'd tell them to *get real*. Yet, here we are." She lifted her head. "It's the middle of the afternoon and we are still close enough not to know where you begin and I end."

Chase took Becca's hand and placed it over her heart. "It beats for you and you alone," she whispered. "I've never felt this close to anyone before. Please, never leave me."

"I can't. Don't you know that?"

"Yes, I can feel you deep inside of me and I know you will never leave me. Nor will I you."

Becca's stomach growled.

"Are you hungry? We should eat something."

Becca wiggled her eyebrows. "Oh, really? What did you have in mind?"

Chase rolled Becca on top of her and they began their dance again.

†

The watcher waited until eleven Wednesday night for Becca to return home. In all the time spent watching Becca, she was never that late. The universe and the watcher's mind became one as the search for Becca began. It wasn't long before the watcher saw Becca in the arms of Chase as they made love.

It is as it should be.

Instead of going home after climbing down the ladder, the watcher walked toward the house. Georgie welcomed the watcher who let her outside. Once Georgie returned inside, her bowl of food and water were full. "I don't think she will be home tonight, girl, so I'll be back in the morning to make sure you get outside."

The watcher walked toward home whistling a happy tune.

†

Becca woke with a start and looked at the clock radio—it was five-thirty. She knew it wasn't in the late afternoon but the morning. With her arms stretched above her head, she smiled remembering the day and night of hedonistic love she and Chase made. Becca looked around the room then to the vacant space beside her on the bed. It wasn't her bedroom. "Chase?"

Chase came into the room and smiled. "Good morning." She handed Becca a cup of coffee. "Black right?"

"Yes, thank you." Becca pushed herself up so her back was resting against the headboard and took the offered drink. "You're so beautiful. How long have you been awake?

"Long enough to make coffee and iron your suit. The beauty of no one consequential seeing you yesterday, is that you can wear the same outfit and no one will be the wiser."

"Crap" Becca's eyes widened. "I need to go home. I left a note to make sure Georgie had food and water and went outside before Gwen left. By now Georgie will be anxious to go outside."

"You've never left Georgie at home alone

"Well, yes I have." Becca looked at the floor. "When my mom passed Georgette had to stay by herself for a day and a half."

"How did she manage?"

Becca shrugged. "I really don't know. When I came home, Georgie ran up to me and I held her as I cried. I guess I let her outside and fed her but it was all such a blur that I have no memory other than Georgie being a comfort to me."

Chase encased Becca in her loving arms. "Want me to go with you?

Becca shook her head. "We can't both be late again. It would put your job in jeopardy and I will not let that happen no matter how much I'd want you with me."

"What about your housekeeper. Doesn't she have a key? You could call her."

"No, I can't." Becca put her coffee mug down. "I'm sorry. I need to go."

"Not yet," Chase said as she too put her coffee mug on the nightstand and kissed Becca's neck.

"God, you are making this so difficult for me, Chase. I have to go now...I just can't let Georgie be there by herself any longer." Becca looked into Chase's eyes. "I need to go...I'm sorry."

Chase smiled. "Nothing to be sorry for, Becca. Actually, I think that your devotion to your pet is an admirable trait." She hugged Becca close then grinned. "You better get going or I might not be able to let you go."

"I'll make it up to you, promise."

"And I won't let you forget that promise." Chase tapped Becca's nose. "Get dressed, go take care of your dog, and I will see you later at work."

†

The watcher was just about to come out from the cover of the trees when the sound of a vehicle's tires rumbling down the road filled the air. After taking a step backward into a denser part of the tree cover, the watcher stood stock still glad for making the decision to wear the camouflage pants and shirt along with a hat. *That was a close one…a few seconds later and she would have spotted me.*

With great interest, the watcher saw Becca fly out of her car and run full speed to the front door. When she had disappeared inside the house, the watcher scrambled up the ladder of the deer stand and began listening.

"Georgie, I am so sorry. I bet you've had your legs crossed all night. Come on, girl, I'll let you outside while I take a quick shower."

The watcher smiled. *She's had a good time. That's marvelous.* Hearing Becca's next words made the watcher grin from ear to ear.

"Joyce, hi, it's Becca…listen, I'm going to be a bit late I am having some problems with my dog and don't want to leave her until I know she is all right…I'll call you as soon as I'm on my way in…any problems I should know about?…Great, I will see you within the hour."

"Good for you, Becca. You're finally taking charge of your destiny," the watcher whispered. *I'd better get going while I can.*

†

Becca pulled her truck out of the shed and headed for the road. Just as she was about to make a right turn she frowned. A person she had never seen before was making their way across her property. She pressed on the brakes and leaned out the window.

"Excuse me, this is private property, and if you paid attention to the signs, there is no hunting allowed."

The person turned and looked Becca straight in the eyes. "So sorry, I was merely taking a shortcut home."

Becca thought the person was so androgynous in padded camouflage pants and shirt that it made it impossible to say definitively whether it was male or female. A camouflage black watch cap covered the head so thoroughly that it was impossible to discern the hair color although the dark eyebrows were an indication.

The trespasser raised both hands. "No weapon. I don't like to kill anything and besides, I'm a vegetarian."

Becca tried to stifle the laughter that threatened to bubble up. "Ok, just be careful. There are several mean bulls roaming the land."

The stranger nodded and turned to continue across the pasture.

Becca laughed the whole way to the road. "A vegetarian indeed. How could I argue against that?"

She chuckled and made a left turn onto the road.

†

It was eight-thirty and the elevator doors slid open on the sixteenth floor of Eastman Industries. Chase Hunter stepped out with a grim look on her face. With long strides, she made her way down the hallway toward Becca Cameron's office. After several soft raps, Chase pounded the door and when there was no answer, she used her master key to unlock the door. The office was dark and the blinds were drawn shut.

Chase left the room, slammed the door, and went to the next office. She knocked on the door and opened it immediately.

Joyce Weston was on the phone. "I'll call you back," she said and hung up. "Ms. Hunter, is there something I can do for you?"

"Where the hell is Cameron? We had scheduled a breakfast meeting for an hour ago."

"Um, Ms. Hunter, Becca called me around seven-thirty and said her dog was sick and she'd be late."

"Did she happen to mention to let me know since she was already thirty minutes late for my meeting with her?"

Joyce swallowed hard. "Her dog is the world to her and I'm sure she is worried about Georgie."

"Isn't that perfect! Her dog takes priority." Chase balled her fingers. "Get on the phone and get the rest of the team out here right now."

All the members of the team gathered outside of Joyce's office.

Chase saw the looks on their faces—fear. She was certain her voice was loud enough to carry to all their offices. "I'd like to know if any of you other than Joyce here knows why Ms. Cameron isn't in her office."

All the team members kept their mouths shut.

"No one knows?" Chase searched all their faces and saw they did not know.

"Ms. Hunter," a soft voice behind her said. "I'm sorry I am late…I had no other choice. Please come into my office and not take out my forgetfulness on Joyce or the team."

Chase turned around quickly and faced Becca. "You were expected in my office more than an hour ago. Instead of alerting me about your lateness you called someone else and did not have the wherewithal to have Joyce here relay that information."

"Please, Ms. Hunter, come into my office so we can talk in private and not out here in the corridor."

"Fine," Chase growled.

†

Chase pushed the door closed and locked it. "What do you have to say for yourself, Ms. Cameron." Her voice boomed around the room.

Becca smiled. "I'm sorry." She moved closer to Chase and wrapped her arms around her. "Whatever can I do to make it up to you?"

"This." Chase kissed her cheek. "And, this." She let her lips brush Becca's before kissing her passionately. "I missed you the moment you left."

"I had to keep a firm grip on the steering wheel and not turn around." Becca grinned. "You should have gone into acting. Did you see the look on Joyce's face?"

Chase nodded. "Yeah, I thought she might cry at one point. We will have to think of something subtle to do for her. To her credit she stuck up for you."

"Joyce is a true gem. She does her work, thinks outside the box on everything, speaks up when she needs to, and is loyal."

"Guess I shouldn't have picked on her like that."

"I think it is safe to say that if anyone of them had a suspicion about us being a couple they don't anymore."

"It was hard for me to act like that." Chase frowned.

"I know. It isn't your style or who you are." Becca tightened her grip and snuggled close to her lover.

Chase could feel her body react to the feel of Becca's body. "I want you."

"I'm yours."

Without a word, Chase moved so that her thigh was between Becca's legs. When Becca began to grind against her Chase did the same. It wasn't long before they gasped into one another's mouths as one's orgasm, then the other's reached a peak before tumbling in ecstasy.

"God, I don't think we can be alone at work again," Becca whispered.

"I refuse to do that." Chase breathed deeply and nipped at Becca's ear. "I don't think I can go a day without seeing you."

"Any plans for the weekend?"

"You, me, and Georgie at your place."

"I like the sound of that."

Becca's phone rang.

"Don't answer it," Chase whispered.

"It's Joyce. She knows I am in here with you." Becca picked up the receiver. "Cameron... No, I'm not... will come speak with you when I've finished with Ms. Hunter... Okay, thanks."

"She wanted to know if you were safe in here with me right?" Chase wiggled her eyebrows.

"Yes, she did. She said it got awfully quiet and she was worried."

Chase caressed Becca's cheek. "Are you finished with me?"

"Not by a long shot." Becca caressed the protruding nipple showing through Chase's top with her fingers. "I don't think I will ever be done with you."

Chase grinned then shook her head. Her phone was vibrating in her pocket. She looked quickly at the message. "As much as I want to stay here and play with you I do have a meeting I must attend."

"We are at work so I guess that should be our main objective."

After a deep passionate kiss, Chase moved away from Becca. "What if I packed a bag and came to your place and spent the night?"

"I'd say you should pack enough and stay until Monday morning."

"You sure? That's a big step."

"I know but I've been waiting all my life for you, Chase, and I don't want to waste a minute of time not being with you when I can."

"Good answer." Chase looked at her watch. "I'd better go or I'll be late." She gave Becca another quick kiss then moved to leave the office.

"Wait," Becca said as she moved close to Chase and tucked in her shirt and smoothed the material where she had twisted Chase's nipple. "There you go, you are now presentable."

Chase opened the door and turned to Becca. "I hope that I will never have to be last on your list when it comes to your meetings with me."

She turned, went out the door, and closed it firmly.

†

Becca heard a soft knock on her door and adjusted her clothes. "Come in."

Joyce stuck her head in the door. "I am so sorry I didn't let her know you'd be late. Thank, God, she didn't fire you."

"It took some doing, but I finally got her to see why Georgie is so important to me."

"You always do know how to get yourself out of a jam." Joyce chuckled.

"Ms. Hunter told me Mr. Douglas is going to take Rick Ross' position starting after his two week vacation."

"What about his job? Are you going to get it?"

Becca shook her head. "All I know is that they have two of the VP's searching for a new manager. They are encouraging those of us at Eastman to consider applying for the job." Becca frowned. "They sent the memo out this past Monday. Didn't you get a copy?"

"I did but I don't think I have the credentials yet to do a managerial job. Once I get my advanced degree then I will submit my name."

"Don't cut yourself short, Joyce. You are an excellent worker and have a very good grasp on how things run. Why don't you apply and see what happens."

"Are you going to apply?"

"No, I don't think I will. For now, I am happy where I am."

"Now who's selling themselves short?"

"Too much is going on in my life right now and the last thing I need is the added pressure being a manager will bring to my table."

Joyce nodded. "Can I get you anything? Did you have breakfast?"

"I'm good. Thanks for asking." Becca patted the pile of papers on her desk. "It never seems to go down. Will you pass along to the team that I'd like to meet with them around one this afternoon?"

"Of course. Meeting room two?"

Becca nodded then watched Joyce leave her office closing the door softly behind her.

Becca, Becca what have you gotten yourself into? She grinned. *Exactly where I belong and need to be.*

✝

Becca was deep in thought about the information she'd received about the new project. It looked like it would take some long hours to make it work. A sharp rap on her door had her looking up. "Come in."

Chase stood in the doorway with an angry expression. "Care to explain this?" She held up a piece of paper.

"If you let me know what *this* is then I can tell you. At the moment it is just a piece of paper."

Chase walked into the room and slapped the paper in front of Becca. "Why did you do something this ridiculous?"

Becca briefly looked at the document and knew instantly what was upsetting Chase. "I'm not ready to be a manager, Chase."

She held her hand up to stop Chase from speaking. "By being the temporary manager, I have realized that it isn't the job for me. To be honest, I haven't had enough experience to do the job properly. We can say all kinds of things about Mr. Douglas but he did know the job."

"You did all his work, Becca, and that more than qualifies you for the position."

"The team may have done the ground work but I had no idea what he was doing and because now that I know all that the job involves, I don't feel comfortable as a manager. Maybe in a few years I'll be ready but not now." She shrugged. "I have too much to learn."

"So you wrote the search committee and withdrew your name without even discussing it with me?" Chase sat in the seat next to Becca's desk. "Why didn't you ask me instead of blindsiding me like this?"

Becca could hear the hurt sound in Chase's voice and if she could turn back the time she would have talked with Chase about it first. "I'm sorry. I should have spoken with you before I sent this out."

She rubbed her forehead that was suddenly throbbing. "I thought I was doing right for myself and our relationship."

"Just what does our relationship have to do with anything?" Chase asked.

"If I was promoted to a manager then I would have to throw myself into the job to learn everything I needed to make the grade." A slight smile curled her lips. "I didn't want to do that, Chase. It would take me away from spending time with you," Becca whispered. "I've waited too long for you to come into my life. You are far too important to me to spend any more time than is necessary away from you."

Chase stood then closed the door and locked it. "Becca, this would have been a great career move for you. You deserve it."

"The only reason I come to work now is to see you and be with you. I don't need the money never have…but I do need you in my life. I just took this job because my mom told me I needed to get out there and make friends."

Chase held out her hand and pulled Becca from her chair. "I never thought I'd say this…but you are the reason I come to work too." Chase kissed Becca's cheek. "I'm sorry that I never asked you if you wanted a managerial position. Instead of assuming, I should have asked you first."

"No matter, the search team accepted my wishes and took me off the list."

Their kiss was slow and tender. When they broke apart, their foreheads rested against one other.

"I need to go," Chase said in a husky voice. "I'm leaving early to go home and pack a bag with enough clothes to stay until Monday morning. Then I will head toward your house."

"Sounds like a good plan to me. Will you text me when you get to your apartment and I will leave for home then?" Becca lightly kissed Chase's lips. "You'd better go or I might have to take advantage of you."

Chase kissed Becca's nose. "See you later."

†

The watcher arrived home and told of the meeting with Becca Cameron.

"You did what? You know that is against all the rules. Secrecy and stealth is how we handle things. The number one rule is *no contact*. What part of that don't you understand?"

"I had no choice. Becca saw me and stopped to tell me I was on private property and there was no hunting on her land. What did you want me to do…ignore her and disappear in a puff of smoke?"

"I suppose she saw your face?" asked one of the others sitting across the table.

"Once again, I had no choice. She seemed more amused than angry and after I was certain she was gone I went into the house and made sure everything I put there was still in place."

"Was it?" another asked.

"Yes, of course it was. I didn't realize she'd be out of the house as quick as she was. Had I, I would have stayed in the cover of the woods. I just wanted to get here as fast as possible and tell you the news about Becca and Chase."

"And that is?"

"I already told you that they spent the night together. And from the tune I heard Becca humming I'd say it was a very successful union."

"That still doesn't excuse your lack of covertness."

The watcher's head dropped. "We are so close. Please do not replace me. Not now. I know Becca better than anyone here."

"Very well but know if you make another stupid blunder you *will* be replaced."

"Thank you."

Chapter Eighteen

The second Friday in November, Becca drove her truck into the shed. The air had a chill to it and the overcast clouds were an ominous blue. She opened the front door just as snow started to fall. Becca turned off the beeping alarm before bending down and giving Georgie a hug and a warm greeting. Without moving from the door, she pulled out her cell to check for calls.

The instant Becca closed her phone it rang. "Hello… I wanted to let you know it is snowing out here… are you going to be able to make it?" Becca smiled. "Wild horses you say? Well then, I will be on the lookout for you… see you soon. Bye."

Becca grinned. She and Chase had spent the past month and a half together at Becca's home and their relationship had become a solid commitment to one another. She looked down at Georgie who was sitting by her feet. "Let's get you outside and then I need to get our supper ready."

✝

An hour later, Chase's car slid into Becca's drive and stopped. Before Chase could get out of her vehicle, she saw Becca running toward her only to slip and fall onto the slick, snowy ground. Without hesitation, Chase was out of the car and moving toward her fallen girlfriend. "Are you okay? Did you hurt yourself?"

Becca was laughing. "Only my pride. How were the roads?" She took Chase's extended hand and stood.

"You should have seen it. Cars were off the road in ditches, I saw one that was flipped...."

"Oh, my God. Was anyone hurt?"

"No. The guy was standing by his vehicle. I stopped to see if he needed help but he'd already called his wife and a tow truck. Needless to say, I took it slow." Chase gathered Becca in her arms. "So why are you out here without your coat on and skating on the ice?"

Becca blew out a breath. "I was so worried about you that I've been watching for you to arrive. My heart was beating a mile a minute until I saw your headlights." She returned the hug and kissed Chase's cheek. "Come on, I'll help you carry your things into the house. I have a pot of soup on the stove and some fresh bread for supper."

"That sounds delicious. My stomach was grumbling all the way here."

Becca's face held a crooked smile as she looked at Chase.

"What?"

"I'm so glad you're here. I have a fire going in the front room and in our bedroom."

"Then let's get inside. It's freezing out here."

Hand and hand, Chase and Becca walked into house where Georgie welcomed them.

✝

Late that night, naked and in front of the fireplace, they snuggled in happy contentment.

"Tell me about your day." Becca said.

"Kellerman and Polanski have narrowed the search for the new manager to two candidates." Chase's eyes twinkled in the firelight.

"Any names?"

"Wish I knew so I could tell you but since I removed myself from the selection committee no one is speaking to me. But if I were to speculate…you'd be in the mix had you not removed yourself from consideration."

"Do you know how much easier it is for us with me out of the mix? If I was a manager that would make you my direct boss and I think that would be difficult for our personal relationship." Becca kissed Chase's cheek. "Before I would ever let that happen, I would have looked for a job elsewhere."

"As much as I would have liked to see you in a managerial position I understand what you're saying." Chase took her fingers and traced Becca's face carefully touching her forehead, eyes, cheeks, lips, chin, and neck.

Becca lifted an eyebrow. "Hmm, that feels nice." A shiver coursed through her body.

"I am memorizing your face so when we are apart I will always see how beautiful you are."

"You won't lose me, Chase. I'm not going anywhere." Becca cupped Chase's cheeks with both her hands. "The first time I heard you speak to me, I felt it in my heart. And the first time you kissed me, your kiss seared my soul. You...." Becca's lips lightly touched Chase's. "Make my heart beat strong and the soul I thought I surely lacked, is full of you."

Chase kissed Becca and pulled her close. "I think it applies to us both."

"I've never been happier and it is all because of you," Becca whispered.

With a serious expression on her face, Chase cleared her throat. "Thanksgiving is coming up soon. Do you have any plans? I mean do you do something special?"

"I vaguely remember a time or two that we went to my grandparent's home. But for the most part it was just the three of us." Becca lifted a shoulder. "Then it was just mom and me and then just me."

"Would you like to go to Wisconsin with me and meet my family?"

Becca swallowed hard. "I would feel like a fish out of water."

Chase's brow creased. "Why? They are really nice people."

Becca shook her head. "Not what I mean."

"Then what?"

"You have eight siblings and they are all married right?"

"Yes."

"Do they all have kids?"

"All but one."

"How many?"

"Hmm, let me see…nineteen." Chase's face brightened. "Oh, I see what you're getting at. You wouldn't know what to do around all those people during a holiday celebration."

"Exactly. Besides, I don't want them comparing me to your other girlfriends."

Chase shook her head. "Becca, I've never taken anyone home with me. They know I'm a lesbian but have never met anyone I dated because no one was that important to me."

"How uncomfortable do you think that would make them all feel? Would they look at me and elbow one another and say—*my God, there's more than one of them.*"

As hard as she tried, Chase couldn't keep her laugh down and soon Becca was laughing as well.

"Let's talk about this more tomorrow." Chase stood and held her hand out. "Come on, let's go to bed."

✝

Chase's eyes opened and she looked at Becca who was snuggled up against her naked body. *God, she's beautiful. How did I get so lucky to have her come into my life?*

"You know I can see you and hear what you're thinking," Becca's sleepy voice said.

"Really, so tell me, mind reader, what am I thinking?"

"Easy, you're wondering how you got so lucky."

Chase grinned. "You are indeed a mind reader. How did you know?"

"It's what I think every time I see you." Becca stretched her arms above her head. "Good morning. Last night was spectacular, as usual."

"And, we have all weekend to explore one another's body more fully." Chase grinned. "That doggie door you had installed sure has helped us stay in bed longer."

"Thanks for the great idea. In the past it wasn't a problem getting up and letting her out." Becca grinned. "But now as long as you're in bed with me I want to stay right where I am."

At that moment, Georgie came bounding into the room.

"You will have to wait a little while, girl, I have to take care of your mom first." Chase ruffled Georgie's head.

"I like the sound of that. Just what do you have planned?" Becca rolled so she was lying on top of Chase and kissed her soundly. When she heard a rumble, she laughed. "Soup and bread didn't sustain you, did it?"

"If you will look at the clock you'll see it is almost eleven."

"That late, huh. I don't know about you but I thoroughly enjoyed making love with you into the wee hours of the morning." Becca rolled off Chase. "Let me get a shower and then I'll make breakfast, although at this hour it is more like brunch."

Chase narrowed her eyes and let a predatory look pass between her and Becca "My back needs to be washed. Any idea how I can get that to happen?"

Becca crooked a finger. "Come with me and I will make sure you are squeaky clean when I'm done."

†

Becca, humming a happy tune, flipped a pancake. She was watching Georgie romp in the snow while Chase was gathering whatever eggs there were. Winter wasn't the ideal time of the year for chickens to lay their eggs. She turned back to the stove and moved the frying bacon around with a fork. The backdoor opened and Georgie came dashing in, skidding across the tile floor with her wet paws. Becca laughed.

Chase entered the kitchen next and placed the egg basket on the counter. "Only three eggs today." She looked up to see Becca smiling at her. "Aren't you in a good mood this morning?" Her arms encircled Becca's waist before she kissed the back of her neck. "The shower was inspiring. It just keeps getting better and better doesn't it?"

"Yes, it does." Becca turned in Chase's arms and kissed her lightly. "Almost done. Will you pour the juice?" She plated the pancakes and bacon smiling at her lover.

"Yep, I'm on it but first…" Chase captured Becca's lips. The phone rang and Becca pulled back, frozen in place.

"Want me to get that? Chase looked at Becca curiously.

"No. Don't answer it…let it go to the machine."

"Bec, you're trembling. What's wrong?"

The phone stopped ringing when the answering machine kicked in and then disconnected.

185

"Becca, what's wrong? Please tell me what's going on."

"I was so happy when you arrived yesterday evening that I totally forgot what happened until the phone rang."

"You had another one of those static calls?" Chase pulled Becca close.

"Yes, on my way home last night. I hadn't received any of those calls in so long I had forgotten all about them." Becca stared into Chase's eyes. "This one started out with static and just as I was about to end the call I heard a voice as clear as a bell."

"What did the voice say?"

Becca swallowed. "It said, *Becca, you must come to me now.*" She shivered. "Then it went back to static."

"Did it happen around the flashing light again?"

"Yes, just as I passed under it."

Chase took Becca's hand and led her to the table. "Sit, I'll get the plates, juice, and food. Then, we can talk about this more and decide the best course of action. Is that okay with you?"

Becca nodded as she sat in a chair. "I'm scared."

Once she had everything on the table, Chase sat next to Becca and gave her a hug. "We will figure this one out. Trust me on that."

"I do." Becca pushed the food around on her plate.

"You told me that you've always been fascinated with Hanging Tree Lane, right," Chase said, as they ate.

Becca nodded.

"The answer has to be there. Do you agree?"

"Yes, and that terrifies me."

"Why?"

"With a name like that, the place must be full of evil."

Chase shrugged. "Not necessarily. Maybe it is a place of justice."

Becca lifted a shoulder. "I guess it could be construed like that."

With Becca's hand in hers, Chase kissed it gently. "We need to go check it out. It is still very cold and there is about two inches of snow on the ground so we don't have to worry too much about potholes."

Becca laughed. "You are a goof. The snow will give way to the pothole with the weight of the truck."

Chase grinned. "Ah, then you are agreeable to checking out Hanging Tree Lane?"

"You're going with me, right?"

"Wherever you go, I will go."

"I won't be as scared with you by my side."

"I think we should take some sort of weapon. Did your dad have a gun safe?

Becca's eyes opened wide. "Do you really think that will be necessary?"

"You're being naïve if you think this isn't a dangerous situation, Bec."

"You're right, of course. Whoever it is has been harassing me for months with the calls." Becca put her hand to her mouth. "Oh my, God, you're right. We need to arm ourselves. The gun safe is in the back of my closet." Becca stood and rummaged in a drawer, then pulled out a key. "Here's the key. There are shells in there too. I think we should take the shotgun."

"I agree. Are there pistols in the safe too?"

Chase got up, pulled a drawer open, and took out a pen and a pad of paper.

"What are you doing?" Becca asked.

"Writing a note about where we are going and why."

"No one will miss us until Wednesday when Gwen comes. I'll call Kim and tell her we are going out to explore Hanging Tree Lane and if I don't call her by tomorrow morning she should call the police."

"Won't she be curious as to why?"

"I've already told her about the static phone calls."

"Okay. I'll get the weapons we will need. Then we'd better dress warmly just in case we need to abandon the truck."

"Good idea."

†

Becca was dialing Kim's number when Chase walked back into the kitchen with a shotgun in her hand. "I'll put this on speaker."

Chase placed the shotgun on the table and nodded.

"Well this is a pleasant surprise. I thought you were spending the weekend with that tall good looking vice president of yours," Kim said.

"I am she's right here listening to our conversation." Becca dipped her hand into sudsy water and pulled out a plate.

"Shit."

Becca laughed. "Nothing to worry about, Kim. Chase *is* tall and beautiful."

"And I'm not offended," Chase added.

Kim laughed. "Good thing. What are you two up to today?"

"Chase and I are going to explore Hanging Tree Lane." Becca heard an audible gasp from her friend.

"Is that wise? Every time I drive by there I get the willies."

"I got another call yesterday and I clearly heard someone say, *Becca, you must come to me now*. Needless to say, I'm scared but I feel safe with Chase so we are going to go there and see if there is anything there."

"Promise you'll call me when you get back home."

"I promise but if it's late I will call you in the morning."

"Nope. If you don't call me, no matter how late it is, I'll call the police and drive out there myself."

"I will call you as soon as we find out what's going on." Becca smiled. "What are you doing today other than laundry?"

"Heather and I are going out on our second date."

"Oh, Kim, that is wonderful. I'm so glad you two hit it off."

"Thanks, so am I."

"I'll call you when we get back."

"Be careful…both of you."

"We will," Becca and Chase said in unison.

†

An hour later, Becca's truck was cruising down the road toward the flashing light and Hanging Tree Lane.

"You know I love the snow when it is around my house." Becca's voice resounded around the interior of the truck's cab. "It is so pristine and untouched. But out here on the road, it is nothing but a whitish brown color that turns every vehicle into a big white blob."

Chase nodded. "Yeah, I know what you mean." She could hear the fear in Becca's words as she spoke about the snow. Chase reached and squeezed Becca's knee. "We are in this together and as long as we are, then nothing will break or come between us. You are safe with me."

Becca smiled a half smile. "I do feel safe with you. It's just that what is waiting ahead for us is unknown and that scares me."

She flicked on the blinker and waited for two cars to pass before she turned into Hanging Tree Lane. She put the truck in neutral then shifted the control button for four-wheel drive. "Well here we go."

The road was smoother than Chase would have imagined. She'd seen the lane in the daylight without snow and it definitely had deep ruts. "There's a house ahead."

Becca slowed down and the truck crept by the run down home. "There's smoke coming out of the chimney so I guess someone lives there."

"We've gone what, a half mile or so?" Chase looked at the place and the words to *This Old House* began singing in her head—the house needed a new roof and a good paint job along with new windows. "It certainly is in disrepair. Let's keep going and see what we find next."

Becca nodded and continued the slow pace she'd set for driving down the road. "That house was in shambles but it didn't look threatening to me."

"Me either. It didn't look like that place even had electricity. But the smoke tells us that someone lives there." Chase gave the house a cursory glance once more. "I don't see any kind of antenna though. Considering the kind of calls you've received, I'd expect to see something like that or a power line leading to the house."

As the truck continued down the lane, trees suddenly sprung up on either side of the road to such an extent that there was barely enough room for the truck.

"I'd say it is time to turn around but the only way to do that is to back the truck up," Becca said.

Chase noted the nervous high pitch of Becca's voice. "But it is beautiful here, isn't it."

Becca stopped the truck and looked at the trees laden with snow blending with snow covering the ground. "Aspen and ponderosa pines mostly. It's so silent and serene. I can't imagine anything sinister or evil here."

"Look." Chase pointed at a deer with its nose deep in the snow. "If this is the type of area that surrounds the person who called you then I don't think you have anything to fear. It's far too beautiful."

Becca stepped on the gas pedal and the truck skidded before moving forward. The dense wooded area gave way to a field that looked like it was once cultivated. The road also got wider—there was no sign of another dwelling. When they reached the end of the lane, both women gasped.

"That's the largest oak tree I've ever seen," Becca said.

"Look at that branch on the far side. Is that a noose?"

Without a word, Becca got out of the truck and began trekking through the snow-covered ground.

"Hey, Bec, wait up." Chase ran as fast as the snow allowed her to and easily caught up to Becca. "No going off alone. Isn't that what we agreed?"

Becca nodded. "Look," she pointed to the noose, "It is real. Wonder who it's for."

Chase felt a shiver go up her spine and pulled Becca close. "Let's go home."

"Not yet. Maybe some local put that there to add mystery to the name of this road." Becca took out her phone and took pictures of the noose and the huge tree. "How old do you think this tree is?"

Chase was directing Becca back toward the truck. "Don't know. Probably two hundred years I guess. Come on, let's get out of here. This place is giving me the creeps."

There was just enough room for Becca to turn the truck around and begin the trek back to the road. "We've gone exactly two and a half miles since we started down this lane."

"Stop," Chase screamed when she spied a stooped old woman with thinning white hair standing in the road ahead.

Chapter Nineteen

Becca clutched her jacket over her heart. "I almost hit her." Her eyes widened. A shotgun's barrel was pointing at the ground. "She's got a gun!"

"At least it isn't in a shooting position." Chase felt under the seat and took the revolver out.

"You're not going to shoot her, are you?" Becca asked.

"No, I'm just protecting us. She has a weapon, which means we should have one too."

The old woman beckoned them to her with a crooked finger.

Chase opened her door. "Come on, we came here for answers and maybe she has them."

Becca cautiously opened the door and stepped into the snow.

"What do you want," Chase asked positioning herself in front of Becca.

A gloved hand pointed at them. "I want her."

"No, she will not go with you." Chase straightened her back making her seem like a bigger threat. "If you will get out of the road we will be on our way."

"You're that Cameron girl aren't you?'

Becca peeked out from behind Chase. "How do you know that?"

"I knew your great granddaddy and great grandma. Helped them build that house you live in."

"Impossible. That would make you more than…."

"I'm a hundred and twelve."

Chase looked skeptically at the woman. *She certainly is old but more than a hundred? I seriously doubt that.*

"Why do you doubt me, Chase Hunter?"

"How do you know my name?" Chase put a protective arm around Becca who had moved beside her. "Are you the one that has been harassing my friend?"

"Is that what she is? Just your friend?" the ancient voice asked.

"That is none of your business, nor is Becca. Now, I asked you nicely to let us pass. Please don't make me regret that."

"My name is Opal Hosmer and Becca is my responsibility. I promised her great granddaddy that I'd watch out for her." Piercing dark cloudy eyes fixed on Becca and Chase. "You might as well come on in, get warm, and have some coffee."

Becca looked at Chase, sending her a silent message.

"I think not, Mrs. Hosmer," Chase said.

Becca and Chase turned around and started back to the truck. The sound of the barrel of the shotgun snapping into place stopped them.

"Around these parts it is impolite to walk away when you're invited in for coffee. You both need to come with me."

Chase and Becca turned around.

"You can put your weapon back in the truck, Chase. It will be useless to you."

"If it is useless then there is no reason to put it in the truck, is there." It wasn't a question. "All we want is to go on our way in peace." Chase moved toward the old woman until the shotgun was against her stomach. Her voice lowered to a growl. "Why are you harassing my friend? She has done nothing to you. I suggest you walk away."

Opal's eyes fixed on Becca. "I promised your great granddaddy I would always watch over his family and that is what I intend to do. Please come in the house and sit by the fire so we can talk."

Chase turned her head. "It's up to you, Becca, what do you want to do. Either way, I am in it with you."

"We came here for answers so we might as well go inside."

Opal lowered the shotgun and trudged through the snow toward the run down house.

"Weren't you afraid she'd shoot you?"

Chase smiled. "No, when she had the barrel open I saw there were no shells in the shotgun."

"I knew I'd always be safe with you from the very first time we met." Becca hooked her hand in Chase's arm. "You still have the gun right?"

"Yep."

"Then let's see if we can get some answers."

✝

Once inside, Becca looked around the interior of the home. Unlike the outside, the inside was warm, comfortable, and well cared for. "Have you always lived here Mrs. Hosmer?

Opal pointed to the huge table that sat in the kitchen. "Take a seat and make yourself comfortable while I fix coffee."

"I don't think I'll drink any of her coffee. My gut tells me she means no harm but I still don't trust her," Chase whispered. "This is all too weird."

"I agree." Becca looked at the woman whose back was to them. "This table is enormous. I've counted ten chairs yet the old woman seems to live here alone. I see no sign of anyone else being here. Let's just find out the answers that we came here for and then make a quick getaway." She rubbed her arms. "There's something about this place that gives me the creeps."

Chase nodded. "I noticed that too. It smells like death to me."

Opal appeared behind them and placed two mugs of steaming coffee on the table. "That'll warm you up right quick." She moved slowly around the table and sat across from her two visitors. "You need not worry about the drink. It is nothing but coffee."

Becca nodded and lifted the cup to her lips. "It tastes good. Will you please tell me why you wanted me to come here? I assume it was you."

"Yes it was me and the others."

"Others?" Chase gave Opal a critical look. "How many?"

"You will find that out soon enough," Opal said. "Becca what do you know of your great grandparents?"

"All I know is that my great grandpa built the house I live in."

Opal folded her hands on the table. "My family was the first to settle in this valley. When your great granddaddy came here with his bride—you look, so much like her—he sat in this very kitchen and told us he wanted to build a big house and fill all the rooms with kids. We all pitched in to build the house. I helped and even carved my name in the north most rafters in the attic."

Suspicious, Chase asked, "How old were you then?"

"Let's see." Opal ran her aged fingers across her lined face. "I was about five at the time. Back in those days, no one mollycoddled the kids like they do today. The adults treated them the same as everyone else. So, I pitched in and did what I could. I filled cans with nails as I recall."

"Then what happened?" Becca couldn't stop her stomach from roiling. "After they built the house that is."

"They waited for a baby." Opal's eyes focused on the window behind Chase and Becca. "It wasn't until five years later that your grandmother was born. The birth was difficult and Louise couldn't have any more children. It broke her heart but she poured all the love she had into your Grandma Bess. Both of them doted on her and I've never seen a happier child."

As if she was in a daze, Opal didn't speak for a long time. "I was with each of them when they passed. It was then that I promised I would always watch for Bess and any family that she might have."

"How old were you then?" Becca asked.

"Well, let's see…I was twenty-five with a houseful of my own. I was a healer by then and everyone sought me out because of the healing powers of my herbs. No one came to get me, but I knew your great granddaddy was ready to leave this earth so I went to the house. I held his hand as he looked into my eyes and asked me to promise that I'd watch over Louise and Bess. I gave him my solemn promise that I would and I did."

"How much time passed before my great grandmother Louise passed?"

"Not long. Six months. She told me as I held her hand that she didn't want to leave Bess alone and I told her I would take her in as my own." Opal looked at the two untouched coffee cups. "Wasn't the coffee to your liking?"

"It is good." Chase said. "I just forgot about it when I became engrossed in your story. It is fascinating." She rubbed Becca's thigh and Becca placed a hand over hers.

"I can remember my Granny Bess and Granddad Carl but it's not clear."

Opal clapped her hands and her voice became brighter. "I never seen two people so much in love as Bess and Carl. They took to one another like peas in a pod. They were true soul mates and after they married, they moved into Bess' house. Carl's parents disowned him for marrying out of his social standing but he didn't care because he had Bess and she was his everything."

"They only had one child too. Right?"

"Bess miscarried five times before your ma was born. The two adored their daughter and gave her everything. Unfortunately, Bess never had another child." Opal tapped a finger to her nose. "It was history repeating itself, I remember thinking."

"What did you do to keep your promise and watch over them?" Becca asked in a soft voice.

"I always knew what was happening with them so they were never very far from me." Opal let out a long sigh. "I kept my promises and watched out for all of you. I was there just before your father passed and he asked me to watch over you and your…."

"Liar!" Becca slammed her hand on the table and moved her chair back with such force that it fell to the floor. "I was the one who was with him. I was the one who brought him back to life not you. When he died in the hospital both my mother and I were there." She pointed a finger at Opal. "*You* were *not* there."

"You really had me going there for a minute, Mrs. Hosmer. Believing the unbelievable. But, just like all liars you tripped yourself up." Chase stood and put her arm around Becca. "Let's go home and be finished with this nonsense."

"Sit back down." Opal's voice boomed through the air. "I haven't finished yet."

"But we have," Chase said softly. "What on earth has Becca ever done to you for you to treat her in this manner?

"In what manner? Watching her? Keeping her safe? Bringing the two of you together?"

Chase laughed. "You brought us together? You honestly think you can take credit for that too?"

Cold eyes pierced both Becca and Chase. "I said, sit down."

They both looked at one another and sat.

"Your father died in the operating room and I held his hand as he let go of his life. His final words to me were, *please take care of my girls, and keep them safe.*"

"How did you know he called us *his girls?*" Becca's voice was but a whisper as she looked at Opal. "Who told you that?"

"Your father did, my dear. He didn't want to leave you but it was time and he entrusted me with your lives."

Becca shivered uncontrollably. "No. No, that can't be."

"It is all true." Opal reached across the table and held Becca's hand. "And, I was there when your mother had her stroke, when she started to fall off the ladder I caught her. That is why there was no bruising on her body."

"Nooo," wailed Becca.

"Stop this! Stop it right now, old woman. I will not allow you to go on with your outlandish tales that you only tell so you can harm Becca." Chase stood and placed both her palms on the table and leaned toward Opal. "Enough."

Opal looked past Chase and focused on Becca. "Your mother begged me to help you find happiness, Becca. She didn't want to leave you alone. When she saw your father beckoning her she knew she had to go. I left Georgette with her to guard her until you came home."

"No one knows that except Chase and Kim." Becca gave Opal a look of amazement. "You were really there? How?"

"Yes, I was there. The how is unimportant."

There was a tap on the back door before it opened. Five women dressed in what looked like flour sack dresses entered the house.

Chapter Twenty

"Who are these people?" Chase demanded. "They look like they all should be in sittin' around shucking corn."

"All will be revealed in time. Have patience, child. Don't be in such a hurry. Take the time to look and listen and you will know all." Opal's voice was strong and brooked no argument. "These are my children. The tall one who came in first is Jessie, our watcher. Then the one next to her is Doris who is our remote watcher. Jean, my youngest, took the alchemy from me and does wonders with herbs and spices. The next, Glenda, coordinates all our activities. Finally, Marge, is my right hand in rescues."

Chase's eyes studied each person as Opal related what their names were and what they did. She looked at Becca. "Isn't that the same Doris I took in?" she whispered.

Becca's body was trembling. "Yes, and the first one that came in was the person who I stopped when she was crossing my pasture."

With narrowed eyes, Chase focused directly on Doris. "I took you in and fed you and made sure you had clean clothes to wear along with a safe place to sleep. I let you get near me. I trusted you. Was it all a ruse?"

In a voice that had an ethereal note to it, Doris said, "I am no fraud. I was doing what was needed to protect you until you met your soul mate."

"That is none of your business. You duped me into thinking you needed help when all along you were nothing more than a snoop." Chase growled at the woman.

Becca noticed Chase's strong emotions and shook off her fear. "You," she pointed to the woman who she met crossing her property, "Why were you really on my property?"

The watcher's clear translucent blue eyes looked away. "It was my job to watch you and keep you safe. You were so fragile, lost, and alone after your mother passed that we feared you would slip into a deep depression and never return."

"You spied on me?" Becca gnashed her molars waiting for an answer.

"I prefer to think of it as watching out for you."

"We had identified your soul mate some time ago and you needed to find one another." Opal's eyes rested on Chase. "You were a lost soul too and by taking Doris in and caring for her you opened your heart. That is what we needed so you would recognize who Becca was when you saw her. No harm was done."

She turned her eyes to focus on Becca. "Nor did harm come to you, my sweet Becca. You needed the combination of herbs that Jean came up with to settle your mind and allow you to sleep."

Becca's voice rose in anger as she glared at Opal. "You drugged me?"

"No," Jessie the watcher responded. "I merely put a sachet of herbs under your mattress. We tried many different ingredients until we found to most effective one. The rest of the time I was in the deer stand watching you."

With eyes wide, Becca turned to Chase. "This is unbelievable."

Becca whipped her head around to glare at the watcher. "You broke into my house and then watched me. How dare any of you invade my privacy like that."

"Didn't you start to sleep without nightmares just before you met with Chase for the first time?"

Becca thought back and nodded. "That doesn't give you the right to break into my house and spy on me."

"I distinctly heard you singing after that. Your heart was no longer heavy and you allowed it to open to the possibility of letting someone in."

"Still, you had no right…no right at all."

"I think we've heard enough." Chase touched Becca's hand. "Haven't we?"

Becca nodded. "More than enough."

Opal raised a hand. "Not yet."

"Why should we stay and continue to listen to this preposterous story?" Chase asked.

Opal reached across, took one of Becca and Chase's hands and held them together. "You both had no light in your souls. They were dark and cold but when you met and gazed into one another's eyes, you looked through the darkness and saw the light igniting in your souls. You saw the light that only a soul mate can bring to its other half."

Becca looked at their joined hands with Opal's covering them. She felt the cold that was permeating the old woman's hand. She had felt that same cold when she kissed her father and mother goodbye after their deaths.

For someone as old as she is it's probably due to poor circulation.

"Are you all for real or am I just dreaming that this is happening?"

Opal glanced at the joined hands then pulled her hand back. "You are not dreaming, my child." She looked at Glenda. "Will you please put some more wood on the fire, I'm getting cold."

Glenda stood, walked around the table to the fireplace and added two logs to the smoldering wood in the fireplace. "That should warm you up in no time, Mama. I was getting a bit cold myself."

"Thank you, child. We cannot let our guests get a chill after I told them they would warm up if they came inside."

"This is all too much to comprehend." Becca looked at Jessie the watcher. "For my entire life you have been spying on me?"

"I prefer watching to that of being a spy. Spying indicates I was interfering into your life. You lived the life you chose and in no way did I try to alter that except to add a sachet of herbs between your mattress and box spring so you wouldn't have those nightmares any longer."

Becca blew out a breath with her eyes focusing on Opal. "What happens now that I know about you?"

"Now that you and Chase have found one another, you are in the safety of one another and will not need us as much. We will always be near if you need us. Of course, when you have your daughters, Becca, we will all be there to keep them safe and happy."

"Daughters? How can that be?"

"They will complete both of you and bind you to one another for all time. For it will be your blood, Becca, coursing through them keeping the blood of the ancients intact. They will be a catalyst that will change the world. Of that I am sure."

"That is preposterous." Chase stood and rested her hand on Becca's shoulder. "We are just at the beginning of our relationship. How can you possibly know if either of us wants children?"

"You will live together in the house built for many children." There was a sparkle in Opal's cloudy old eyes. "Together you will build a family full of love and happiness and when the time comes, we will be with you. Your lives together will be rich and happy. You will thrive in the love you share."

"It's getting dark." Chase took Becca's hand in hers. "We need to go."

Becca nodded.

"Before you go," Jean the alchemist said. "Let me get you a sachet to hang in the north window of your bedroom."

"For what?" Becca's eyes narrowed.

"To keep you safe. What else would it be for?" Jean asked.

"After what we've seen and heard today it could be for anything, even something sinister." Becca stood and squeezed Chase's hand.

"Sinister? How can you say that? Have we hurt you in any way?" Opal's voice became stronger. "Our only intention was to keep you safe, child. Evil is not what my children and I are about. I am highly insulted that you would say such a thing."

"With all that you revealed to us today, what would you all think if you were in our shoes right now?"

All the eyes opposite Becca and Chase focused on them. "We'd say *thank you*," they all said in unison.

"For what? You were apparently watching my every move and sent Doris into Chase's world to spy on her. Should we be thankful for the deceit and manipulation?"

Becca shook her head. "You told me that you were there for all the matriarchs and patriarchs who passed in my family since my great grandfather. I find that incredulous yet you've revealed things that no one else but a select few know. I am having a hard time getting my head around it all."

Becca let her eyes rest on each woman across from her for a moment. "I need time to digest it all before I can consider thanking you."

Jean deposited a sachet of herbs on the table in front of Becca. "Put it in the north window of your bedroom."

Becca picked up the item and shook her head. "I want to believe but it is so hard to make sense of it all."

"Faith is what carries us all through our lives, Becca. If you do not have faith in something then your life will be meaningless," the watcher said. "We have given both of you a great gift. Do not squander it or let it die. Embrace the love that you feel and find happiness in one another for that is all we've asked or ever wanted for you."

At that moment, Becca felt a strong kinship to Jessie the watcher. It was as though she'd known the woman all her life.

In a way, I guess I have.

She rested a hand over her heart and nodded. "And that is all I've ever wanted in my life."

Chase smiled at Becca. "It is what I have been looking for all my life and have found in you." She looked at Opal. "We have a lot of information to digest and as I said, it is getting dark. May we visit you again?"

Opal shook her head. "I think not. We have never revealed ourselves before and it is with great peril that we did today."

"Great peril you say…why is that?"

"We have broken the fundamental rule that we live by and that will have consequences."

"Not because of me, I hope." Becca gave Chase a nervous glance. "Perhaps we should have just stayed in the house today and not followed my desire to drive down Hanging Tree Lane. If I have put any of you in jeopardy, please let me know how I can fix that."

"You did what your heart told you was right, child. It was our choice to reveal ourselves to you." Opal smiled fondly at both Becca and Chase. "Be on your way and live in love."

"We will," Becca said as Chase nodded.

It was as if an impenetrable force was leading them to the door and the truck. And before either Becca or Chase knew it, they were back at Becca's house.

Chapter Twenty-one

"Is it just me or do you too feel like you've just woken from a dream?" Becca asked as they walked toward the house.

"It's not just you. I felt it the minute we walked inside that place. It was like I was there but wasn't…really creepy." Chase put her arm around Becca's shoulders. "It is easy enough to check out part of the story."

"How?"

"We go to the northern most corner of the attic and see if we find a name carved in the wood."

"Do you have any idea how cold it is in the attic this time of the year?"

"You forget that I grew up in Wisconsin, so yes, I do know how cold it is. If we find Opal's name then we know that at least that part of her story was the truth."

"What about the rest of it?

"We can look in the deer stand and see if anyone has been in there recently."

Becca looked at the structure. "Let's go there first." Becca returned to the truck, opened the door, and took out a flashlight. "This will come in handy."

Together, Becca and Chase walked the short distance to the deer stand.

"Want me to go first." Chase wrapped her fingers around a shoulder high rung of the ladder.

Becca passed the flashlight to her lover. "Yes, but just go up there and once you can see what's there then come back down."

A crooked smile crossed Chase's lips before she scampered up the ladder. From high up she said, "It looks like someone has been here recently. I can see faint footprints like whoever was here had on wet boots."

"It could be a vagrant looking for a place out of the cold." Becca looked up at Chase's feet as they disappeared into the deer stand. "Hey, going inside wasn't part of the bargain."

"I know but I just wanted to look around a bit more. I'm on my way down now."

"What do you think?"

"Someone has definitely been up there recently. Was it Jessie the watcher? There is no evidence that it was her if that is what you're asking."

"But there was no evidence that she wasn't."

"Exactly." Chase descended and wrapped her arm around Becca's shoulders. "Come on, you're shivering. Let's get inside and get a fire going to warm us up."

"Sounds good to me. My brain is fried with all these revelations." Becca leaned into Chase.

"Do you want children," she asked as they walked toward the house.

"Never really thought about it." Chase shrugged. "I like kids. Babies especially. I'd worry that our lifestyle might impact them negatively with others."

"Good point," Becca said opening the front door and punching in the code for the alarm. "Hey, Georgie girl, did you think we never were coming back?"

"If Jessie really came in the house, I wonder what Georgie did."

"My guess…she brought her a treat." Becca laughed. "Give her a treat and she'll be your friend for life."

Chase pursed her lips. "Yeah, that would stand to reason. Let's go see if there is a sachet of herbs in the bed."

"Why don't I heat up some of that soup from yesterday and you get a fire started in here first. If there is something in the bed it will still be there."

"No, I want to put this to rest, Becca. I can see all of this rattled you. Having soup and a fire isn't going to change that. If we find the sachet then we know that Jessie's story is true."

Becca looked nervously at the stairs. "If it's there, then what?"

"Then we check out the attic. Other than that we have nothing else to go on." Chase pulled Becca close and kissed her on the cheek. "We are in this together."

Becca took comfort in Chase's words. "Then let's go find out the truth."

Chase stopped on the first step. "First you need to call Kim before she sends out the police."

Becca pulled her cell from her back pocket and pressed Kim's speed dial number. "Hey, Kim, I am calling to tell you we are back at our house. There was nothing at Hanging Tree Lane but an enormous oak tree. Talk to you later. Bye."

"Why didn't you tell her what we found?" Chase asked.

"I hated omitting what happened but something is telling me that I need to keep it just between you and me."

Chase wrapped her arm around Becca's waist. "I have the same feeling. It was all so bizarre and surreal, yet my heart tells me they meant us no harm."

"Still, it is hard to digest. It reminds me of an episode from the *X-Files.* "

"I loved that series. " Chase grinned. "Let's go see if there is anything under your mattress or in the attic."

†

"Glad we still have our coats on." Becca stood by Chase and they lifted the mattress. "It's there right where she said it would be."

"Are you sure you never put anything like that there or maybe someone else did when they were visiting you." Chase gave Becca an earnest look.

Becca shook her head.

"Okay, let's go up to the attic."

"Wait, do you still have that flashlight?"

Chase nodded.

"There are lights up there but I doubt they are strong enough to show anything on the rafters." Becca pulled open the drawer for the nightstand and pulled out a large flashlight. "This, along with the one you have should give us all the light we need."

The door to the attic squeaked when it opened. "I hope there aren't any bats or rodents living up here," Chase said as she climbed the stairs.

"You're not alone in that," Becca quipped as she flipped the switch for the lights. "Surely while growing up on the farm you went into rooms only to find something scurrying to hide."

"Yet another reason I didn't want to stay on the farm." Chase grinned. "I didn't see anything moving when the lights went on so maybe we are safe from critters."

The dust and cobwebs told Becca that no one had been in the attic in some time. She remembered playing in there when she was around ten. She looked around as unbidden memories flooded her mind. With her hand, she swatted at tears that threatened to fall.

"Are you okay?" Chase lifted Becca's chin. "It's all too much for you, isn't it?"

Becca nodded. "I didn't realize how many memories were stored just above my head. I remember being up here with both my parents." She sighed. "Never mind, let's go to that corner." Becca pointed at the northern corner. "She did say north right?"

"Yes." Chase took Becca's hand as they walked toward the place where Opal said she carved her name."

Becca turned on her flashlight as did Chase and they began running their lights up and down the rafters. "Do you see anything?"

"Not yet. Once we've checked this side, we need to look on the other side. If she was five when she carved her name, it will be on the lower edges of the rafters. I can't imagine her tall enough to carve higher than four feet."

"I agree." Becca flashed her light along the edge of the rafter and stopped near the wall. "Look there," she said.

Chase looked and moved her flashlight to join Becca's beam of light. She ran her fingers along the wood. "Come closer with your light."

With trepidation, Becca moved closer to where Chase had her hand. "What do you see?"

Chase was bending her head to get a better look at what was on the rafter. "O-P-A-L." She looked at Becca. "It's her name."

Becca shook her head. "I…I…she was telling the truth. What do we do now?"

"We get the fires started and have the soup you made along with bread and wine. We can discuss a strategy while we eat." Chase took Becca's hand and led her to the stairs.

"I think we will need to write down what we know is fact and that which we have no proof of."

"Good idea." Once they were back in the hall Chase shivered. "I sure am glad we're out of the attic."

†

The kitchen was warm and welcoming as Becca and Chase sat with their heads together as Becca added salient points on a pad of paper. The list had all the names of Opal's children and what they recalled were their jobs concerning both Becca and Chase.

"Okay, we know Opal did carve her name in the rafter." Becca wrote that down.

"And that someone was in the deer stand," Chase added. "Oh, and let's not forget the herb sachet under the mattress."

"Got it." Becca tapped the pen next to Opal's name. "We have no way of knowing whether Opal was with my decedents at their passing or not." Becca tapped the pen again. "But she knew that Georgie rested her head on my mother's body. Only you and Kim know that."

"Do you buy the part about being with your father?"

"That's hard to say. Surely if someone like Opal was there, I'd have noticed."

"You would think." Chase placed her hand over Becca's hand to still the tapping. "What about Doris? I have to admit I did find peace in her presence." Chase shrugged. "But that could just be because I was feeling good about helping her."

"Did helping her make you feel that way or was it just a natural thing to do?"

Chase shrugged again. "I never really thought about it. When I first saw her, she seemed to be in dire circumstances and to me that shouldn't happen to anyone, so I helped her." Chase's brow furrowed. "I remember thinking how icy cold her hands felt when I helped her into the warmth of the building. All I wanted to do was to comfort her. No. I was compelled to help her like I had no choice."

"So it is possible that part of the puzzle is true."

"Yes, I agree. I never really thought about Doris as anything other than a lost soul." Chase frowned. "Sort of like me."

"And me." Becca put the pen down and looked out at the deer stand. "Opal was right, you know."

"About what?"

"The light in my soul coming to life when I first saw you."

"For me too." Chase hugged Becca. "What do you say we clean up the dishes and go to bed?"

"Good idea. I feel like I've been through a wringer and my nerves are frazzled."

In silence, they carried their dishes to the sink, rinsed them, and put them in the dishwasher.

"Finished." Becca pulled Chase to her and kissed her lips. "But not with you."

"I like the sound of that." Chase grinned. "Shall we lock up and go to our bed?"

"Yes. Let me bank the fire first and we will go to bed and not think of Opal or her children until the morning."

"Agreed. I think that in the morning we will be able to look at what has happened with new eyes. We can go through the list again and then go back to Opal's house and ask her any questions we may have."

Becca watched as Chase poked the burning embers before adding more wood.

"That should keep the room warm until the morning."

"Yes it will."

Hand in hand, they began climbing the staircase.

"She told us not to come back. Can we risk making her angry?" Becca looked directly at Chase. "I guess if we want answers, we really don't have any other choice."

"There is nothing Opal or her children can do to us now, Bec. Our lives are where they should be—as one."

"Don't you worry about upsetting the apple cart? If Opal indeed did all she said then we have to view her as a formidable force."

"She may be, but I will never let anything come between us. We have free will and that she cannot take that away from us ever."

Becca yawned as they reached the top of the stairs. "I am tired but not so tired that I don't feel the desperate need to be one with you."

"You read my mind."

✝

Chase and Becca lounged in bed late into the morning. Their lovemaking when they woke was slow and deliberate. Each touch, caress, and kiss reaffirmed their inextricable bond with one another for life.

"I love you, Becca," Chase whispered. "I've never been as sure of anything in my life."

Becca kissed Chase passionately. "I love you too. I feel so unbelievably lucky to have you in my life. I was an empty shell destined, I thought, for a solitary life. The last thing I ever expected was to find you. The love you've brought into what was my unhappy guilt-ridden life was so unexpected and welcomed, all at the same time."

"I'm pretty sure that I loved you from the moment I first saw you but it wasn't until you came into my office that I realized how I really felt about you. It scared me, Bec, and I wanted to run as far away from you as I could get. It was later when I saw Doris quietly eating in the reception area and I realized that I didn't want to become her and be alone for the rest of my life." Chase softly kissed Becca's cheek. "Maybe, just maybe, that is why she was there."

"That is one of the questions we will have to ask Opal."

"Once we clear things with her we can start thinking of sharing our lives on a more permanent basis."

Becca grinned and held up her index finger before opening the nightstand drawer. She pulled out a small box with a ribbon. "I was planning on giving this to you yesterday but we got so involved with Opal that I lost track of it." She held out the box to Chase.

Chase took the box with a quizzical look on her face. "What is it?"

"Open it and find out." The smile on Becca's face was that of a small child at Christmas.

"Oh, Becca," Chase said after she lifted to top off the box.

"Would you like to move in here with me and Georgie?"

As if on cue, Georgie came bounding in the room and jumped on the bed.

"I'd love to. Is this sort of like the lesbian and the U-Haul?"

Becca laughed. "No, we've been together too long for that old story."

"What do you say to grabbing some breakfast, looking at the list, and visiting Opal again? Once we clear that up there will be nothing standing in our way."

Chapter Twenty-two

"I don't know about you, but saying I'm nervous would be an understatement," Becca said as she made the turn to get on Hanging Tree Lane. "I think we should ask her how this road got its name, don't you?"

"Yeah, I'd be interested in finding that out too. If anyone would know it would be Opal."

Becca's truck slowed as it came to the house before it stopped in the middle of the road.

"It looks like it snowed last night. I can't see our tire tracks from yesterday."

"I didn't notice it at your house so it must have been a localized snow shower." Chase looked at the house and pointed. "Do you remember the house looking that disheveled?"

Becca glanced in the direction of the house. "To be honest, I wasn't paying much attention to the house yesterday. My head was spinning with ideas of what we'd find. Come on let's go see what Opal has to say for herself today."

The snow crunched under their feet as Becca and Chase walked to the house, climbed the three steps, and knocked on the door. The motion made the door swing open.

"Hello, Opal, you in there? It's Becca Cameron. I was here yesterday with Chase Hunter. We'd like to speak with you if we can."

Chase pushed the door open wider and whistled. The interior of the house was in disarray full of broken furniture, dust, and cobwebs. As they carefully walked farther inside, they gaped at what was the table they sat at the day before.

Becca let out a yelp as a mouse skittered across the floor. "This is too weird. Pinch me so I know this isn't a dream."

Chase took off her gloves and lightly pinched Becca's cheek.

"Ow. Okay, we aren't in some sort of dreamscape. We *were* here yesterday right?"

"Yes, we were."

"Then how do we explain this?" Becca was gesturing with her hand across the house. "She said we couldn't come back, do you think this is why? Could what we saw yesterday be some sort of holographic image?"

"What do we have here?" Chase moved closer to the broken table, saw an envelope with Becca's name on the floor, and bent to pick it up. "It has your name on it."

Becca ripped the envelope open and took out a single sheet of notepaper.

"What does it say?"

Becca, you were both told not to come back. Knowing your inquisitive nature, I knew you would not heed my words. You will find nothing here for you and there never will be again. It is for your own good that you do not pursue this further. You have all the answers if you will just open your mind to the universe and listen to what it tells you. The Watcher, Jessie.

Becca's eyes scanned the note again. "What do you make of it, Chase? Is there some clue we've missed?"

"*You have all the answers.* What do Opal, Jessie and Doris have in common? They are the ones we came in contact with while the others were just bit players to us."

Chase looked perplexed. "I feel like it is staring us in the face."

"It has to be something inconsequential that we didn't think was important. Like the facial features, a touch, or a word they all have in common."

Becca thought for a moment then her eyes flew wide open. "Didn't you say that when you first found Doris her hands were ice cold?"

"Yes, they were cold and waxy feeling."

"That is exactly how Opal's hand felt on mine yesterday and I remember thinking her hand felt like my mother's face when I kissed her goodbye before I buried her. Is that what you felt too when her hand covered both of ours?"

"You're right. Wow! Did you notice that even though you could see color, all their eyes looked as if they had cataracts?"

Becca placed her hand over her mouth. "Oh my, God. Are you thinking what I am?"

Chase swallowed hard. "It can't be…can it?"

"The only way to find out is to research Opal. We know approximately when she was born."

"Great idea. My mom used to do all this genealogy stuff and I helped her some. I know the sites we can go to." Chase grinned. "Are you game?"

Becca nodded.

†

The ride back to Becca's home was one of quiet reflection.

Once out of the truck and inside the house, Becca shivered as she held onto Chase. "I have to admit that all of this scares me."

Chase kissed Becca's cheek. "I know but unless we at least try to find out it will always haunt us." She stepped back and looked directly into Becca's eyes. "You do want to know don't you?"

Becca nodded. "Yes I do."

"Then let's go fire up your computer and see what we can find."

Becca thought for a minute. "There's this gentleman, Frank Hathaway, who is ninety-eight and his mind is still sharp but his hearing is failing him. We could visit him and see if he remembers Opal and her family."

Chase looked at her watch. "It's one-thirty now. Do you think we can visit him today?"

"Yes, I believe we can. He is my housekeeper's grandfather and he lives with her and her family." Becca, pulling her phone out of her pocket, quickly dialed the number before pressing the speaker button.

"Hello, Gwen, it is Becca. How is your day going?"

"Becca this is an unexpected surprise. To answer your question, my day is going great. I've got dinner in the slow cooker and just sat down to read a new novel I bought while the chocolate chip cookies I made are baking."

"Sounds like you have everything under control at your house. Listen, I'm calling you because I'm looking into my family's history and that of those living around the time my great grandparents came to the area."

"You'll love doing it. About five years ago, I did the same thing and found out some interesting things about where my folk's families came from. I can give you the name of all the sites I used."

"Fantastic. What I'm hoping to find is what their lives were like all those years ago. Do you think my friend Chase and I can visit with your dad and find out what he remembers about the time when my great grandparents,

grandparents, and my mom and dad lived in this house?" Becca squeezed Chase's hand.

"Of course you can. Dad was just telling me this morning that he'd be glad when the snow was gone so his buddies could visit."

"It will be great speaking with him again." Becca laughed. "I can still remember the stories that he told me when I was a kid."

"He is fortunate that he still has full use of his mind. When did you want to come?"

"Is two hours good with you? That will give me time to see what I can find on the Latter-day Saints' web site."

"I'll save some cookies for you."

"I just heard my stomach rumble."

Becca and Gwen both laughed.

"We will see you in a little while then."

"I'll keep an eye out for you. Goodbye."

"Bye bye."

Chase wrapped her arms around Becca's waist and kissed her. "It will be interesting to hear what he has to say."

Becca nodded. "Yes, it will. I need to use the bathroom while you find the site on my computer."

✝

"Okay, here's Opal Miller born in 1901. It doesn't give a date of her death."

Becca pointed to the computer screen. "Click there and see if we can find out more."

Chase clicked the link and soon found some of Opal's family history. "She married Herbert Hosmer in 1916."

"That means she married when she was fifteen. Back then that was not all that unusual."

"Look at this." Chase pointed the cursor at a list of Opal's children. "They are all here. Jessie, Doris, Jean, Glenda, and Marge."

"It looks like she had Jessie when she was sixteen and had the others every year until she was twenty."

Chase clicked on a few more places on the ancestry website. "Herbert died in March of 1922. I have one more place to look" Chase said as she opened another genealogy website. Her fingers glided over the keyboards as she typed in Opal Hosmer then Opal Miller—nothing. "That's weird. The Latter Day Saints genealogy site was always my mom's go to place when she couldn't find what she needed and it had nothing more than she was married and have five girls. This site has the same information."

"Maybe Gwen's grandfather can tell us more." Becca looked at the wall clock. "Let's go and see if Frank can give us something to go on."

"We're like regular detectives." Chase grinned then gave Becca a kiss on the cheek. "Does Gwen know about us?"

"You mean that we are lovers?"

"Yes."

"No. Our relationship has nothing to do with Gwen. She cleans my house and when my mom passed away, she was very supportive. My personal life is just that—personal—and it is something she has no need of knowing about." Becca shrugged. "As I told you before, I have very few friends who I share my life with."

She wrapped her arm around Chase's waist. "Come on let's go. I feel like doing some sleuthing. Besides once you move in she will quickly know that we are lovers."

†

The interior of Gwen's house was in a word, comfortable.

"Hi, Gwen," Becca said with a bright smile. "This is my friend Chase Hunter."

Chase extended her hand and Gwen took it. "It's nice to finally meet you in person, Gwen. Becca has nothing but praise for you."

Gwen blushed. "It's a pleasure to meet you, Ms. Hunter."

"Please call me Chase."

"All right, Chase." Gwen's eyes turned to Becca. "Pop is in his room and is expecting you. You might want to take your coats off. He keeps his room very warm." She pointed down the hallway. "It's the second door on the left."

✝

Becca rapped on the open door and smiled when Frank Hathaway looked at her. "Hello, Mr. Hathaway, it's good to see you," she said loudly.

"Becca, my dear, why haven't we seen you in church lately?" He motioned to two chairs. "Please close the door and take a seat."

Becca looked at Chase and winked. "I've had some personal matters to attend to for the past few months."

"Well, don't stay away too long. You wouldn't want God to think you've forgotten him."

"I will. Mr. Hathaway, this is my friend, Chase Hunter."

Frank had a twinkle in his eyes as he looked at Chase. "Friend indeed," he whispered. "Gwen said you wanted to know about the early days of my life and of those who lived here then."

"That's correct. Do you know anything about the Miller family that lived down Hanging Tree Lane?"

Frank rubbed his chin. "Yes, I know of the family."

"Did you know Opal?"

"Opal." His eyes brightened. "Yes, she was much older than me. I knew her daughters Marge and Glenda quite well. We were in the same class in school. It's a pity what happened to their whole family."

"What happened?"

"Well, they didn't go to our church but another one." Frank tapped his forehead. "It was some newfangled type of religion that didn't catch on here. Anyway, after Opal's husband died she took control of the running of their place and she and her girls worked the farm. It was a good little place and they never bothered anyone with problems. They only helped when someone was in need. The only time I remember seeing them as a family was at a school function for raising money so the school house could have a new roof."

Frank stifled a yawn. "Back in those days that's what we did when we needed something for the school."

"Do you know what happened to them, Mr. Hathaway?" Chase asked.

Frank nodded. A sad look crossed his face. "Yes. A week went by and none of Opal's kids came to school so they sent two men out to their place to see if something had happened to them. When they got there, the inside of the house looked—these are their exact words—*like a war zone*. Their furniture lay on the floor tossed about and broken but they didn't find Opal or her girls. It was as if they had disappeared off the face of the earth."

"Did they ever find them?"

"Sadly, yes. About two weeks later, a man who was out hunting found all six of them hanging from the oak tree at the end of the road. Why anyone would want to hurt any of those sweet women baffled everyone. Opal and her girls were always the first ones to help neighbors in need. I remember one time when one of their neighbors' house burned down and they gave them all a place to stay even though space in their house was limited. Opal and her girls all tripled up so their neighbors would have rooms of their own." Frank shook his head. "To this day I can't figure out what they ever did to die that way."

Becca's hand flew to her mouth. "Oh my God, that is awful. Did they find out who did it?"

"No. The state police did an investigation and the newspaper headlines carried the story but after a month that all died down. That is why it has the name Hanging Tree Lane. Originally, it was part of Opal's property but it became a place for people to go and gawk at the tree. The state put in that flashing light after numerous accidents happened on the highway and the road to the tree with people wanting to see where it happened."

"Amazing," Chase said. "And no one ever found out what happened?"

"No. Now it is just part of the folklore of this area."

"Wasn't there any speculation going on as to the why?" Becca asked.

"None that I heard. The folks around these parts at the time were in shock. Opal and her girls were beloved for their kindness. We were a small community back then and only gossiped about who was or wasn't at church and why."

Becca pondered Frank's words. "I've never heard that story before and I've lived in the same house all my life," Becca said.

"By the time you were born, Becca, it was nothing more than a ghost story. No one remembers the story now. There are too many other things competing for people's attention."

"Thank you for sharing the story with us, Mr. Hathaway. I've always been curious about Hanging Tree Lane and we drove down it yesterday."

"Did you see the house?"

"Yes, it was run down but still standing. We went to the end of the lane and saw the oak tree and a lone noose."

"That noose has been there ever since. When time takes its toll and the rope gets rotten, someone always replaces it. No one knows who does that. I reckon that it must be someone that was close to the family. Of course, by now, they'd be old coots like me. Getting that rope over the branch is not an easy task." Frank gazed at the two women curiously as if he were debating what to say.

"Did you see anything or anyone else?" he finally asked.

Chase reached out and took Becca's hand.

"Yes, we spoke with Opal and her girls." Becca whispered not expecting Frank to hear her.

Frank clapped his hands. "I knew it the moment you asked your first question. I remember about thirty years ago I went down the lane on a walk about and thought I saw someone working on a flowerbed near the stairs. I kept going and when I came back, the person was gone so I went to inspect the flowerbed and nothing was there. It didn't look like anyone had touched the dirt in years and there were no flowers. I distinctly remembered seeing a flat of flowers next to the woman. I got up my courage, went to the front door, and knocked. The door pushed open easily and I saw what I thought were the remnants of Opal and her girls' struggle for life."

Frank shook his head. "Needless to say, I got out of there fast. You saw them all. I only saw who I thought was Opal."

Frank scratched his chin. "That very night my first grandchild was born. I took seeing Opal as a sign that something good was coming my way. Don't ask me why I thought that for it just bubbled up and I remembering feeling safe."

"Inside the house everything looked warm and cozy. There was a fire in the fireplace and Opal made us coffee. Everything seemed normal. We did notice that Opal's hand was very cold but chalked that up to her age," Becca said.

"It seems that what we saw was some sort of an illusion." Chase smiled at the older man.

"After hearing your story, Mr. Hathaway, I think what we saw were guardian angels." Becca sighed in contentment.

Both Becca and Chase stood.

"Thank you for speaking with us, Mr. Hathaway. At least now we know we aren't the only ones who have seen them." Chase held her hand out and Frank shook it.

Frank stood, walked to the door, and opened it. "You are both welcome here any time."

†

"That was interesting," Chase said as she got into the truck.

"Yes, it was. I guess now we know what we saw weren't real flesh and blood people."

Becca started the truck. "What's next?"

"We continue our lives together. For whatever reason, Opal and her children conspired to bring us together." Chase rested her hand on Becca's thigh. "I know you are the one for me. If guardian angels had a hand in helping us find one another, then so be it."

"I like the idea of angels bringing us together." Becca leaned in and kissed Chase's cheek. "Let's get home and make plans for your move to the country."

Chase smiled. "Once we get settled in, will you marry me and come home with me and meet my family."

"Yes, to marrying you and maybe to the family."

"Ah, but, it's a package deal since they will all be at our wedding."

"Okay, I am warming to the idea."

"Good answer." Chase fastened her seatbelt. "Let's go home."

✝

Both Becca and Chase took time off from work the three days before Thanksgiving. They were making the final check of Chase's apartment on Monday to make sure they had moved everything to the farm. When Chase's cell rang, it echoed around the empty room and startled them both.

"Hello… Hi, Mom. What's up... Really... How long... Yes, she's here with me… Okay, we'll see you then."

"I take it that was your mom," Becca said.

"Yeah. She and my dad will be here in twenty minutes."

Becca's eyes widened. "You mean like right now? I thought we discussed this and I said I wasn't ready to meet them yet."

"Relax. I told them that but my mom insisted on meeting you anyway. They flew in today just so they could meet you." Chase grinned. "They are just like everyone else, Bec."

"Thanksgiving is in three days. Shouldn't your mom be at home making pies or something?"

Chase laughed. "My dad has his pilot's license and they flew here just for the day. While they are visiting us, his plane will be refueled so they can fly back this afternoon."

Becca held her stomach. "I think I'm going to be sick."

"No, you're not. I told my mom about two weeks ago that I'd found *the one*. She asked if I was bringing you for Thanksgiving and that was when I told her that you weren't ready for the big family experience." Chase hugged Becca close. "I could hear the disappointment in her voice and she just told me that they wanted to meet the woman who I finally gave my heart to."

"But, I'm not sure I can…"

There was a knock on the door.

Becca froze.

Chase opened the door and smiled before she hugged her mom and dad. "This is a wonderful surprise."

She turned to Becca. "Mom, Dad, I'd like you to meet my partner, Becca Cameron."

Becca could feel her body trembling but stepped forward and held out her hand. "It's good to meet you, Mr. and Mrs. Hunter."

Chase's mother grinned. "My name is Linda and his is Ben."

She moved forward and engulfed Becca in her arms. "I am so happy to meet the woman who has wooed my girl from her office." Linda stepped back. "Why, my dear, you are shaking like a leaf. I hope it isn't because of us."

Becca took a step back. "I am surprised that you flew all this way to meet me. No one has ever done that before."

She looked at Chase's mother and gave her a slight smile. The woman was shorter than Becca imagined she would be. Linda was on the plump side but Becca saw where Chase got her good looks.

"Well, of course we would, little lady, we've worried about this gal for years wondering if she'd ever settle down. I, for one, am really glad to meet you." Ben winked at her then turned to his daughter. "She is a looker."

Chase blushed. "Dad…."

"Aw come on now. There's no way you can deny how beautiful Becca is." Ben nudged Chase with his elbow. "In fact, I can say of all our daughter-in-laws, she is the best looking."

"Ben, behave yourself. Can't you see that you are embarrassing them both?"

"Indeed." Ben took a step closer to Becca and wrapped her in his arms. "Thank you for making my little girl so happy," he whispered.

"You're welcome," Becca whispered back. "I'm the lucky one."

"What do you say we all go find something to eat and you can all get to know one another better," Chase said.

"Sure sounds like a good idea to me," Ben said. "I could eat a side of beef I'm so hungry."

Becca laughed. *I think I'm going to like him the best,* she thought. "Then let's go."

She turned to Chase. "What about Alfredo's Place?"

"Perfect." Chase hugged Becca. "Thanks."

✝

That night as Becca lay next to a sleeping Chase, she looked out the window to the star laden sky. She liked Chase's parents and knew her life was now complete. Never again would she feel alone in the world, for she not only had Chase but the family that came with her. A star traced a line through the night sky and the sachet in the window caught her attention. She smiled.

Thank you, Opal and your girls, for bringing us this happiness. May you all rest in peace.

Epilogue

"This is so unfair." Meredith stomped her foot and dug in her heels. "Everyone else's parents are letting them go, so why won't you let me?"

"Because I am your mother and I make the rules." Becca countered

"No." Meredith sneered at her mother.

"I'd suggest you change your attitude, young lady, if you ever want to do anything with your friends again."

"Beth, Katie, and Sue are going and all my friends will be there. They will all laugh at me if I don't show up." Meredith wept. "You're ruining my life. I wish I lived anywhere but here."

"Unfortunately, that is not your choice."

"Hey, what's all the shouting about?" Chase asked, coming into the kitchen

"She won't let me go to the party with my friends," Meredith cried. "All I ever wanted to do was be like everyone else. It is bad enough that they laugh at me all the time. It's all her fault. I hate her."

"You will not speak to your mother like that. Is that clear?" Blue eyes the mirror image of Becca's bore into her. "If I had spoken to my mother when I was growing up like you just did—I'd never have seen daylight again. It's time you grew up and started to act like you're fourteen instead of like a two year old."

A hand went up to forestall argument. "Now apologize to your mother."

"You can't make me." Meredith turned, opened the kitchen door, and ran away from the house as fast as her legs would go.

"What is it with all this drama?" Chase asked.

"I think it is called her monthly teenageritis."

"And we have how many more years of this?"

"I think it extends into the twenties." Becca grinned. "At least that is what your sister Margret told me. Maybe we will get lucky and it will only last till she is eighteen."

"God, help us."

"Hey, what's going on?"

Both Becca and Chase looked at their youngest daughter, Kelly, and shook their heads.

"We have to look forward to this again," Chase said with a smile. "Honey, your sister is upset because we won't let her go to a party that will have no parents present to supervise."

"Well, that's dumb. I guess she wasn't listening when you told the story about doing the same thing and all the trouble you got into."

Chase hugged her daughter. "Well, at least you were listening."

Her eyes tracked to Becca who was standing looking out the window.

†

Meredith, with tears in her eyes, ran blindly away from the house.

"I hate them both," she screamed.

Tears flowed freely as her bare feet ran into rocks, twigs, and anything else that was lying in the worn perimeter road that ran around the property. Anger kept her from feeling the beating her feet were taking.

Meredith stopped running and, looking at where she was, she frowned. Before her was the small pond where her family usually picnicked and swam.

"I hate her." Meredith stomped the ground and instantly cried out. "Ow! That hurts."

She limped to a flat rock, sat, grabbed her right foot, and turned it to examine the cause of the pain—her foot was bleeding.

"What happened to you?"

Alarmed, Meredith looked toward the source of the voice. A very tall woman with hair the color of snow stood a few feet away from her. *Just because it's a woman doesn't mean she won't hurt me.*

Meredith's eyes looked for a way out until she saw the blood on her foot again. *I'll never out run her.*

"I mean you no harm. My name is Jessie and I was just taking a shortcut to my home when I saw you hopping to the rock. I'm pretty good at fixing wounds and can take a look at that nasty cut on your foot."

Meredith backed away from the woman. "My foot is fine." She felt the tremor in her voice as she looked once more for a way out—there was none—the rocks and the woman were penning her in.

Jessie took a step closer. "I won't hurt you. What's your name?"

"Meredith," she whispered.

"I'm pleased to make your acquaintance, Meredith. Do you live around here?" Jessie let out a laugh. "Of course you do why else would be here barefooted."

Jessie smiled and dropped her backpack on the ground next to the rock.

"I...I forgot to put my shoes on when I left the house."

"Had a fight with your mom, did you?"

Meredith's eyes widened. "How do you know that?"

"The tear stains on your cheeks and the fact you have no shoes on gave me a clue." Jessie's voice softened. "I remember when I was about your age and my mother insisted I go out and gather eggs and I didn't want to. So I ran away."

"Where'd you go?"

"Not far. I hid in a big oak tree outside our house. From there I saw my mother searching for me."

"How long did you stay there?"

"I was stubborn and stayed put until I saw the desperation on my mother's face and heard the panic in her voice." Jessie shook her head. "It was then that I realized that I was being a stubborn baby and climbed down the tree."

"Did your mother punish you?"

"No, she kissed me all across my face before pulling me into a tight hug. She said, *I thought I'd lost you, baby.*" Jessie sighed heavily. "Her eyes were glistening just like yours are now and knowing that I was the reason. I hugged her back and told her that I loved her."

"And she didn't punish you?"

"No." Jessie smiled. "She told me she was reminded of a story in the bible—the parable of the lost son—and that she was rejoicing in finding her lost daughter." Jessie grinned. "That night she made me my favorite—custard pie. We didn't have a lot of money back then but she prepared a feast as if we did. It was then that I knew just how deep a mother's love runs. My mother loved me in spite of my hateful words and deeds."

"Oh." Meredith gave the woman a curious look. "Where exactly do you live? I know all the people around here and I don't remember seeing you before."

"I live across the highway. Jessie smiled. "Will you let me look at your foot? It's still bleeding."

Meredith looked at her foot. "What are you going to do to it?" she asked in a tentative voice.

A smiling Jessie pointed her chin at Meredith's foot. "There's lots of dirt and stuff on your foot and that is a perfect breeding ground for germs. I'd like to wash it all off and make sure there isn't anything embedded in the cut."

Once again, Meredith looked for a way out and seeing none, she nodded. "Okay, you can wash it out."

Jessie, squatting near her backpack, unzipped a section and took out a kerchief. "I'm going to get this wet so I can wash off the dirt and gunk."

"Okay." Meredith's eyes never left the woman and she made her way to the edge of the pond.

"That water is really clear so I don't think it will make your wound any worse." Jessie knelt next to Meredith and gently took hold of her injured foot. "Let me know if I hurt you."

Meredith watched Jessie wad up the kerchief and let the water dribble onto her foot.

"Are you okay?"

"Yes."

"Good. Now I'm going to lightly remove the rest of the dirt."

Jessie's touch and manner were soft. Although Meredith still hesitated in trusting the woman, she was grateful for the help Jessie was giving her. Her eyes widened when she saw all the small cuts around one larger one.

"I'm going to wash this out again," Jessie held out the kerchief. "And then rinse your foot again. Is that okay with you, Meredith?"

"Yes, thank you for helping me."

Jessie winked. "It's my pleasure."

After the second washing, it was clear to Meredith that a small rock was still protruding out of the bigger cut. "What about that?"

Jessie's eyes followed Meredith's finger to the rock. "It might hurt when I take it out or I can help you get home so your mom can take you to the doctor."

"No," Meredith barked. "Go ahead and pull it out. How much can a little rock like that hurt?"

"Very well then." Jessie put her thumb and index finger on either side of the rock and instantly jerked it out before wrapping the cloth around Meredith's foot "Are you okay?"

Meredith nodded trying to conceal the tears that the pain caused.

"Hold this tightly and I'll be right back."

With a steady gaze, Meredith watched as Jessie walked around the pond. Every so often, she would stop to stoop and pick something up.

Once she'd gone around the entire pond, Jessie again crouched in front of Meredith's injured foot. "Take the cloth off please."

The voice of the woman was soft and soothing and Meredith began pulling the cloth off immediately.

Jessie wadded what was in her hand and pushed it into the wound.

"What's that?" Meredith asked. "You aren't poisoning me are you?"

Jessie chuckled. "No, it is not poison. It is spider webs that I collected from around the pond."

"Yuck."

"It will stop the bleeding." Jessie waved her hand around the area. "Nature has its own pharmacy, if you know what to look for."

"And you do?"

"Yes, my mother is a master herbalist and she passed that knowledge to all of us."

"All of us?"

"I have four sisters. Jean, the middle child, was the one my mother shared all of what she knew about plants and cures. She in turn taught me what to look for."

"I bet you never screamed *I hate you* to your mom." Meredith looked away.

"That is something that every child does either verbally or mentally."

Meredith lifted her eyes. "Really?"

"Yes, really. What did your dad have to say about what happened between you and your mom?"

"I don't have a dad." Meredith hesitated. "I have two moms."

Jessie nodded. "How do you feel about that?"

Again, Meredith hesitated as she sorted out what she wanted to say to Jessie. *Can I trust her?* She looked to the kind soulful eyes and closed her eyes before speaking again.

"My mom told me that love knows no gender."

"She's right you know."

Meredith nodded. "I know. It's just hard at times."

"Why?"

"Because not everyone is as accepting." Meredith blew out a breath. "There are kids in school that make fun of me and say mean things about my mom's relationship." She chewed on her lip. "Mom told me that if someone does that they aren't really my friend."

"Prejudice comes in all forms, Meredith. Sometimes people say cruel things because they don't understand people who are different from them. Other times, people are mean because their church, parents, or teachers taught them that certain behaviors are wrong and sinful. Tolerance has a very hard time overcoming intolerance."

"Do you think they know how much it hurts when they say awful things about both my mom's relationship?"

"Some probably do and say it because they know they will hurt you. They are just mean spirited. Others probably are mimicking what they've seen others do or say and have no idea how much it is hurting you."

Jessie patted Meredith's leg. "Your job is to have compassion for them for they are truly ignorant of what love is all about. God is all about love."

"But, some tell me God hates me and my mom's for being…um…abhorrent and we are abominations that will go to hell."

"Is that what you believe, Meredith?"

A lone tear rolled out of one of Meredith's eyes. "I don't know. I look at the two of them and see how much love there is between them, my sister, and me. We aren't any of those things."

"Yet, there is doubt." It wasn't a question.

With downcast eyes, Meredith nodded. "I do love them."

Jessie looked at Meredith and could tell she was scared and truly sad for her thoughts against her mother's relationship. It was clear that the girl loved her mother's but others caused the turmoil and self-doubt she was feeling.

"May I sit on the rock with you, Meredith." Jessie purposely kept her voice soft. When she saw the girl nod, Jessie sucked in a deep breath. *Here goes nothing.* "I'll tell you a story, okay?"

"Sure go ahead."

"Back many years ago—it is too many years to remember the actual number—my mother was forced into the role of taking care of her girls alone. You see my father died and she had no choice but to step in and take control."

"Did you hate her for that?"

"No. No, not at all. We were proud of the way she made a life for us all. We were all properly cared for and we went to school with clean clothes every day. While we were at school, she'd tend to the cows and all the business that was needed to run our place and make it profitable."

"She was a strong woman then?"

"Yes, very strong. Some though, thought she was a bit strange because she believed in the power of nature." Jessie breathed deeply. "There was this group of men who would come to our house in the middle of the night and beat on tin pans and shout *witches live here*."

"Didn't your mom call the police and have them arrested?"

Jessie shook her head. "Back then, there was only one policeman for the entire area and he was useless." She shrugged. "The men always seemed to avoid detection by anyone but my family. My mother told us they were harmless and drinking made them act like fools."

"Did your mom know their names?" Meredith wrinkled her forehead.

"Oh, yeah she knew all of them. She said some of them even grew up with her." Jessie looked at the pond then threw a rock into it.

"What happened that made them single out your family?"

"Don't know. I remember one night they came and my mother stood in the doorway and stared at them as she whispered a prayer of forgiveness. One of the men—I think his name was Billy McDermott—somehow swallowed his tongue—so the story goes—and was choking on it. All the others just stared at him and didn't do anything to help so my mother went to him, slapped him on the back really hard a couple of times, and he finally got his breath back."

"They must have been thankful after that and stopped harassing your family."

Jessie smiled and shook her head. "One would think so but it didn't happen that way. The next night they were back but there were only two of them and they were mean old coots who pounded on our door and broke it down, shouting *death to the witches*. I remember them ransacking our house as they tied us all up."

"Did they hurt you?"

"Don't remember. Just woke up the next morning with my mother and all my sisters in a strange place."

Meredith frowned. "I don't understand. Why didn't the police do anything to stop them? Isn't that what their job is?"

Jessie's gaze fell on Meredith's face. "No one knew and no one saw so there was no one to point a finger at who did it."

"Why didn't your mother or you and your sisters tell the police?"

"We couldn't because we were in that strange place and it took a long time to make our way back to our home."

"Weren't you frightened by what was happening?" Meredith's eyes opened wide.

"No, not really. I had my mother there and I knew she would take care of me and keep me safe. When I woke up the next day, I could feel her love surrounding me. It was like a never ending dream and it was then that I realized just how much my mother meant to me."

†

Meredith couldn't stop the flow of tears that began running down her cheeks. The simple woman beside her

237

spoke so passionately about her mother and sisters that Meredith realized she wanted that too.

"I've always felt safe with my mothers and secure in their love for me." She sucked in a deep breath and blew it out. "I can't imagine what it would be like to have someone break into our home. I know both my mom's would do whatever they had to so me and my sister were safe."

"Why the tears then?" Jessie put her arm around Meredith's shoulders and gave her a gentle hug. "From my experience, a mother's love is boundless."

"I know that. I've always known that. Yet I was so mean and hurtful to them in spite of what I know to be true." Meredith sobbed louder. "They will never love me again."

"Do you really believe that, Meredith? That their love is so fleeting that the first time you say hateful things to them they will stop loving you?"

"No, I know they love me."

"How do you know?"

Meredith could feel her tears dry and smiled. "I know it in here." She touched her chest over her heart.

"They loved you enough to let you run away without any shoes on. Do you have any idea how much it took for them not to chase after you to make you put your shoes on?"

"They knew I wouldn't go far, right?"

"Yep, that about sums it up. That and they knew your guardian angel would watch out for you." Jessie reached in her backpack and pulled out a pair of tennis shoes and socks. "Here put these on so you don't hurt your feet any more than you have."

Meredith frowned. "I don't understand. Why do you have new shoes in your backpack?"

"In case of an emergency." Jessie smiled as Meredith put the shoes on. "Now it is time for you to go back and talk with your moms and find a solution that will suit everyone."

"They never listen to me."

"Do you listen to them?"

Meredith had a sheepish look on her face. "Yes…I mean no."

"Then go and speak with them."

"What about the shoes?"

"Keep them."

Meredith looked down the road toward home before turning back to tell Jessie thanks—she was gone.

"Jessie." Meredith called. "Jessie where are you?

Her eyes scanned around the pond and in the field beyond—nothing. Meredith stood and looked at the spot where Jessie's backpack was and saw only dirt. "That's odd. It's almost like she was never here."

The dirt around the front of the rock they sat on was only disturbed by her feet with no sign of Jessie's boots.

From what seemed like a far distance away, Meredith thought she heard someone calling her name.

"Mom."

With feet that no longer hurt, Meredith ran full stop down the dirt road toward her home.

✝

For thirty minutes, Chase and Becca stood at the front windows waiting for their daughter to return home.

"Are you sure we shouldn't look for her," Becca asked.

"We saw her run toward the pond and not toward the road. She'll come home when she's ready." Chase put her arm around her wife's shoulders. "We need to let her feel like she has some control in the situation."

"She's been gone for too long. I'm going to go out and find her or at least call to her."

"Don't go after her, it'll make her feel like a baby."

"I won't" Becca shook her head and went to the front door to open it.

"Meredith, come home it's dinner time," she called.

She looked down the road then sighed when she didn't see her daughter. Once back inside, Becca shook her head. "I'm going to get the beast out and go look for her."

"You don't have to. I see her running this way."

Becca flew out of the door and Meredith flew into her mother's outstretched arms. "Baby, are you okay? I'm so glad you're back."

Meredith buried her face in her mother's chest. "I'm so sorry, Mommy. I don't hate you. I love you."

Becca pulled her daughter in closer and when Chase joined them they all whispered words of love and forgiveness.

"Come on inside," Chase said. We've made your favorite, ham and mac and cheese.'

"Yes, we will all sit together and be glad for having one another in our lives." Becca wrapped her arm around Meredith's waist as they walked up the porch stairs and entered the house.

Kelly joined them.

"I'm so glad you're back, Meredith. The moms were really worried about you," Kelly whispered when she hugged her sister.

Chase stopped suddenly. "Hey, you left the house with bare feet where did you get those shoes and socks?"

"I met the most remarkable person down by the pond."

Becca's eyes widened. "A stranger was on our property and you spoke to him? Did he try to hurt you?"

"No, Mom, it wasn't like that at all and it wasn't a man but a woman."

"A woman?" Chase asked. "What did she look like?"

Becca exchanged a knowing look with Chase.

"Well, she was really tall."

"How tall?" asked Becca.

"She was a very tall woman who had long white hair and the most remarkable voice with a soothing quality."

"Did she have a name?" Chase asked.

"Jessie. She said she was taking a shortcut home and saw me trying to stop my foot from bleeding. At first I was afraid and tried to think of a way to run but I couldn't see a way out."

"Oh, baby, that's awful. I'm sorry we weren't there for you." Becca put a comforting arm around Meredith's shoulders. "It must have been very frightening for you."

"That's just it…I wasn't scared after she started talking to me. She had a handkerchief and used it to wash off my foot before she pulled the rock out."

"Was it deep? Should we take you to the hospital for stitches?" Chase asked.

"No, after she cleaned it she went around the pond and gathered spider webs and put them on the cut. She said it would stop the bleeding and it did."

"Then what happened?" Chase gave Becca a nod knowing exactly who Jessie was.

"Tell us more will you, Meredith."

"Mostly we talked. She told me about growing up with her mom and four sisters. Her mom was a widow and knew all about herbs and remedies. She said some men would come to their house at night and call them witches. But her mom would just look at them and pray for their souls. Then one night only two men came and broke into their house and tied them up."

Becca placed her hand over her mouth.

"She told me she woke up the next day in a different place that was full of love and all her family was around her. It took them a long time to get back home but they did eventually."

"Where does she live?" Becca looked a Chase who was slowly shaking her head.

"She said across the highway."

"So how'd you come across the shoes?" Chase asked.

"Jessie had them in her backpack and said she carried them just in case she might need them. I took the socks and shoes, put them on, and when I looked up to thank her after tying the shoes, she was gone. I looked everywhere for her but I didn't see a trace that she was even sitting there by me." Meredith sucked in a breath. "It was then I heard you calling me, Mom, and I ran all the way home."

Once again, the mothers and daughter hugged and fiercely held on to one another.

✝

That night after Meredith and Kelly went to bed, Chase and Becca lay in their bed holding hands.

"It looks like our girl has a guardian angel in the form of Jessie Hosmer," Becca said smiling.

"Yes, and our girls will always be safe and cared for just like Jessie's family looked after us. I don't think we should ever tell her they were hung, do you?"

"No, I like the idea of them waking up in the midst of family and surrounded by love."

Becca rolled on her side and put her arm around her wife. "Surrounded by love. What a fitting way to live your life."

That night after Chase had drifted off to sleep, Becca went to the window and looked at the deer stand and smiled as she placed her palm on the pane of glass and muttered a quiet prayer of gratitude.

Out in the deer stand the watcher's heart soared.

About the Author

Erin O'Reilly

Erin O'Reilly was first challenged by a friend to write a story. Erin has since written numerous online and published works. Her story *Deception* was a GCLS Finalist in 2008. That book also garnered the Sapphic Readers Award in 2009. Her book *Fearless* was a GCLS finalist in 2012. Story creation, involving strong characters, always seems to dictate the story and invade her mind at all hours. It always amazes her when the characters she is developing suddenly take on a life of their own and lead the story down a completely different path. In her experience, the characters make a powerful impact on the storyline, thereby making the story better.

Other Books from Affinity eBook Press

<u>Beginning of the End</u>—Alane Hotchkin What happens when life doesn't go exactly as you planned and you must protect others from your own fate? Escaping a horrific childhood, Nikki longed to find happily ever after in adulthood. What she found was Hell. Or did it find her? Finding the courage to break the cycle of betrayal, she opens her heart one last time. Alex lived a childhood others dreamed of. Her father never once denied the young rebel a thing. All her life she dreamed of protecting others; to follow in her father's footsteps. Soon though she learned sex and fists made the most powerful of weapons. Alex controls the women in her life through fear and sex, will breaking the cycle be too much to overcome? Will loving Nikki be enough to change her, or is Alex beyond help?

Alex would give Nikki the world, but at what price? When a person's tightly controlled reality snaps what then…? This is the Beginning of the End for one of them and the ultimate sacrifice for the other. But who is who in this game of life?

<u>Galveston 1900: Swept Away</u>—Linda Crist On September 7-8, 1900, the island of Galveston, Texas, was destroyed by a hurricane, or 'tropical cyclone', as it was called in those days. This story is a fictional account of Mattie and Rachel, two women who lived there, and their lives during the time of the 'great storm'. Forced to flee from her family at a young age, Rachel Travis finds a home and livelihood on the island of Galveston. Independent, friendly, and yet often lonely, only one other person knows the dark secret that haunts her. Madeline "Mattie" Crockett is trapped in a loveless marriage, convinced that her fate is sealed. She never dares to dream of true happiness, until Rachel Travis comes walking into her life.   As emotions come to light, the storm of Mattie's marriage converges with the very real hurricane. Can they survive, and build the life they both dream of?

This second edition of one of Linda Crist's best-loved novels maintains the original story, while incorporating some reader-pleasing passages that were cut from the first edition. As an added bonus, the short story "Something to Celebrate" is included at the end of the novel, detailing further adventures of Rachel and Mattie.

Rapture: Sins of the Sinners—A. C. Henley & Fran Heckrotte A serial killer is targeting young lesbians throughout the state of Texas.Texas Ranger Cochetta Lovejoy is assigned to the case. Convinced she knows who is committing the murders, Ranger Lovejoy is willing to do whatever it takes to put the perpetrator behind bars--even if it means stretching the limits of the law by manipulating the judicial system. Detective Agnes Kelly-Elliott is one of Ft. Worth Police Department's finest investigators. When Ranger Lovejoy appears on the crime scene of a recent murder, Agnes fears a dark secret that, if revealed, could destroy her family ties, and end her career. This is a dark, gritty, graphic tale of desire gone awry, and flawed characters looking for redemption in all the wrong places.

Till There Was You—S. Anne Gardner Julia is a woman used to power and is not afraid to use it or impose her will to get her way. She appears to have the world but a part of her is empty and cold as a frozen tundra. Julia rides in the mornings to clear her head and to make plans for what she is about to set in motion. Theodora, known as Teddy, is trying to put together a marriage filled with uncertainties. She felt once upon a time that she would have a great love but that has eluded her. One morning these two women meet and from the first instance, it is explosive. The attraction is undeniable, the fears very real and the end without question will change them both forever.

Denial—Jackie Kennedy Time spent in Somalia has Doctor Celeste Cameron accustomed to living and working in a war zone. Coming back home to America, Celeste is glad to see the end of the peril she has been in—or so she thinks. Danger seems to follow Celeste and she finds it in the shape of Amy. What Celeste feels for Amy scares her more than anything she has faced in war zones. Amy has the same feelings, but is in denial and vows to marry Josh, Celeste's twin brother, no matter what. When fate brings them together again, will they give in to their mutual attraction or will they once again deny what they feel.

In Name Only—JM Dragon - Sequel to The Fix-it Girl Can an agreement forged out of necessity actually work?

'55 Ford—Erin O'Reilly Andrea McBride, the author of four books, wants to find someone to restore an old '55 Ford truck that she inherited in a real estate purchase. She will only settle for the best and finds RJ Whittaker who many proclaim to be the best restorer among millions.

<u>An Affair of Love</u>—S. Anne Gardner From a dark past, a forbidden love, a secret comes. Among the confusion and the chaos of an unwanted reality, two women find something they neither want nor can deny.

<u>Desert Heat</u>—Dannie Marsden For Luce Diamond, an undercover policewoman, her life is in shambles. Her longtime lover left her and an automobile accident that resulted in a child's death haunts her.

<u>Taming the Wolff</u>—Del Robertson ONLY ONE WOMAN...HAS THE POWER...TO TAME THE WOLFF...

<u>Private Dancer</u>—TJ Vertigo Reece Corbett grew up on the mean streets on New York City, abused, used and in trouble with the law. Faith Ashford grew up wealthy, with all the creature comforts that money provides. When they meet fireworks begin.

<u>Miriam and Esther</u>—Sherry Barker Miriam thought her life would play out in the bustling metropolis of Dallas, but after a life-changing accident, she moves to the small town of Cool Lake, Texas to get her head on straight and regain her senses.

<u>McKee</u>—A.C. Henley Private Investigator Quinlan McKee has returned to Los Angeles after a three-year absence, only to find herself embroiled in a world of child slavery and police corruption.

<u>Nocturnes</u>—JD Glass From acclaimed author, JD Glass, and featuring some of her most loved characters. Nocturnes is a collection of events and adventures, from the sensual dreamscape of the deepest love, to the brooding intensity of desire.

<u>Bailey's Run</u>—Ali Spooner Bailey Chambers mourns the loss of her lover, Nessa, in an unsolved carjacking. When Tommy, Bailey's brother becomes a victim of a gay bashing, Bailey assumes his case will be handled the same way as her lover's—lackadaisically.

Desi Dexter assigned to Tommy's case, feels Bailey's disdain toward her and her partner. Through tenacious police work, Desi, is able to uncover the reason for Bailey's attitude, and convinces her that she is sincere in solving the case.

Mutual attraction sparks, and before they can move forward with their fledging romance, Desi, and her partner Braxton, uncover the presence of a serial killer.

What will happen to Bailey, when, Desi, becomes engrossed in another case, can their relationship survive?

E-Books, Print, Free e-books

Visit our website for more publications available
online.

www.affinityebooks.com

Published by Affinity E-Book Press NZ LTD

Canterbury, New Zealand

Registered Company 2517228